The Celestial Child

*'The bird sings not because it has a message
but because it has a song,' said the boy.*

Who is this strange boy that has
arrived in the village?
And how does he know so much?
And where did the dolphin come in?
Led by Sarah, the village children
take the boy to their hearts ...
but tre͏ ͏ ͏ ͏ ͏ews all the same.

Don Conroy

DON CONROY HAS MANY TALENTS and interests – writer, artist, TV presenter, environmentalist and naturalist. He studied art at the National College of Art and Design, Dublin, and worked as a designer and illustrator for several advertising agencies and in the theatre before moving to television. He has studied nature closely, especially owls, and is actively involved in conservation. His books range from wildlife stories and drawing books to wacky stories for younger children. His drawing books show how to draw true-to-life images as well as cartoons of people and animals.

The Celestial Child

Don Conroy

THE O'BRIEN PRESS

DUBLIN

This revised and re-edited edition
first published 1994 by The O'Brien Press Ltd.,
20 Victoria Road, Rathgar, Dublin 6, Ireland.
Tel +353 1 4923333   Fax +353 1 4922777
E-mail books@obrien.ie
Website http://www.obrien.ie

British Library Cataloguing-in-publication Data
Conroy, Don
Celestial Child
I. Title
813.54 [J]

ISBN 0-86278-381-X

The O'Brien Press receives
assistance from

The Arts Council
An Chomhairle Ealaíon

2 3 4 5 6 7 8 9 10
99 00 01 02 03 04 05

Typesetting, editing, layout, design: The O'Brien Press Ltd.
Printing: Cox & Wyman Ltd., Reading

This world of imagination
Is the world of eternity

WILLIAM BLAKE

DEDICATION

For my family and friends

Chapter 1

The boy moved slowly on the surface of the sea. Waves caressed his body with a soft, rhythmic motion. The waters stretched endlessly, bluey-green, as far as the horizon. Above him, wisps of white cloud drifted across a clear blue sky.

He felt refreshed and excited, at once a privileged spectator of the natural world around him and at the same time a part of it. He was at one with the elements – the sea, the wind, the sky, even the clouds.

Was he alone? he wondered. There was so much to know. Was he discovering or remembering? He had seen so much in his dreams and visions, yet there was nothing around him now but the sea and the sky. Somewhat confused but yet enchanted to be here, he lay back in to the waves, letting them take him wherever they chose.

Suddenly, he sensed he was no longer alone. New, strange feelings – of fear and panic – washed over him.

He turned round to swim with deliberate strokes, looking over his shoulder to right and left, but there was nothing to be seen.

From below the surface, liquid black eyes watched the boy's lithe young body above. Then a dorsal fin cut through the water at frightening speed. Hungry, the shark circled, its streamlined body slicing through the waves, tail twitching. Instinctively, the boy sensed danger. He knew he was faced with a threatening creature, supremely confident in its own element, with superior strength and speed. Its entire body was a killing machine, poised ready to strike. Any minute it would attack.

The fin was heading directly towards him. He flung himself to his left, just barely avoiding the shark's snapping mouth. It circled behind him, determined not to miss a second time. The boy shuddered, feeling helpless and alone.

Clear out of the water another creature sprang, twisting its whole body, then crashing down into the sea between the shark and its intended victim. The startled shark turned and dived deep into the water and sped away. Again, the new creature leapt into the air, this time in a more playful mood. It twirled its sleek body, displaying its great acrobatic skill and then slammed back into the turquoise sea, splashing the boy in a shower of frothy spume.

Wiping the salt water from his eyes, the boy began to focus again. He no longer felt any fear, realising there was no danger from this enchanting creature. The dolphin circled the boy curiously, making clicking sounds and gesturing with fluent movements of its head.

The boy immediately recognised the dolphin as a friend. He understood the meaning of the gestures and the clicking noises, taking only a few seconds to tune into the dolphin's language. The dolphin apologised for the shark's behaviour and explained that it was not out of malice, but because of hunger, that the shark had tried to attack him.

Then, realising that the boy was still somewhat shocked and weak after his experience, the dolphin invited him to rest upon its back. The boy gladly accepted, climbing astride the dolphin's back and taking firm hold of the dorsal fin.

Propelling its body forward like a dart, the dolphin moved along the surface of the sea at magical speed, occasionally leaping clear of the water, with the boy holding on tight and laughing loudly in his excitement.

The seas seemed endless. The dolphin showed him the manx shearwaters, flashing their black backs and then turning to reveal their white undersides as they weaved in and out among the waves. It drew his attention to the gannets that circled high above, the dark-brown of the younger birds contrasting with the adult birds' white plumage gleaming in the sunlight.

Folding their black-tipped wings, the older gannets would dive steeply into the sea for fish. Sometimes they needed several attempts to be successful. Sometimes, too, a great marauding skua would chase them through the sky, forcing them to give up their catch.

The boy looked on in wonder at all the different life forms. A large flock of common scoters bobbed up and down on the surface of the water like a black raft. As the dolphin came near, they rose up and flew low over the waves, settling down again some distance away. The dolphin moved tirelessly through the waters and the rhythmic movement lulled the boy into a sleep, though he kept his grip on the dolphin's fin.

*　　　*　　　*

He woke to witness the sun sinking beneath the waves. A few clouds hung in the sky, pink from the sun's rays. The red disk slid slowly down into the shiny, grey water before finally dipping below the horizon. The yellow glow faded from the sky and a dark-blue dusk quickly replaced the fading light.

Stars twinkled in the evening sky. Beautiful music filled the stillness from below, echoing through the hushed waters like a sacred symphony. When the boy asked about the sounds, the dolphin explained that they came from its relations, the humpback whales.

The boy's heart surged with joy as he listened to the haunting melody across the vast ocean. Then the dolphin revealed to him its knowledge of the watery world, of the different creatures in the sky and in the oceans, and the many moods of the weather. Still the boy could not realise how suddenly the weather could change. But as it sped along, the dolphin sensed a subtle shift in the winds and warned the boy of a storm brewing. The whales were silent now. The wisps of cloud in the night sky were replaced by a towering black swirl which covered the stars and heavy thunder-clouds obscured the moon.

Rolling waves began to churn up the calm sea and the wind swelled from a whisper to a roar. The boy was barely able to hold his grip on the body of the dolphin, which seemed to get slippier as the waves swept over it.

The storm did not bother the dolphin but it felt the body of its young companion becoming colder and colder. 'Grip tighter,' it told the boy, knowing that it must soon find shelter for him.

*　　　*　　　*

The storm got worse and the lightning danced on the waves. A clap of thunder startled Sarah from a deep sleep and she sat up in bed. As usual, her window was half-open with the curtains pulled across. She could see the driving rain spattering onto her desk where she kept her books and the small precious dolls which had been given her since she was a baby.

She was now thirteen and she felt both excited and scared by the storm. Suddenly a flash of lightning streaked across the sky, followed by an explosive crack of thunder. Sarah scrambled out of bed to close the window and another streak of lightning lit up her reflection in the window-pane.

It looked so ghost-like that she instinctively jerked back, knocking down her favourite doll. Tears welled up in her eyes as she saw its arm broken. It was the last present she had ever had from her mother. She remembered the night she got it. Her parents had come back from Italy and she had stayed up to welcome them home. Their plane was delayed but she was determined to stay awake so she kept splashing her face with cold water. Even Gran had fallen asleep by the kitchen fire and the younger children, Mary and Jamie, were fast asleep. At last, her mother and father arrived home and had given Sarah her present of a beautiful china doll. She always associated it with her mother, who was to die tragically in a car accident soon after.

Sarah looked into the small mirror beside her bed. Her tears fell freely as she traced with her finger the scar over her right eye which was a permanent reminder of that terrible night.

Out of the corner of her eye Sarah suddenly noticed a movement of light. She glanced out the window. It was not lightning this time, it moved too slowly, and it seemed to illuminate part of the wood, then fade again. That's curious, she thought to herself, wondering what it might be. She hoped no-one was lighting a fire in her Bambi wood, as she called it. Another crash of thunder and Sarah ducked in under the bed-clothes and tried to go back to sleep. The window-frame rattled and the rain beat against the glass. Just as she began to feel drowsy, she heard the dog howling.

Poor Bingo, she thought, as she got out of bed again and tiptoed downstairs. She lifted the latch of the kitchen door, which blew open with the force of the wind. The dog ran in, barked once and shook himself.

'Quiet, Bingo! Oh dear, now I'm sopping wet,' Sarah said as she pushed the door closed. The dog barked again. 'Quiet,' she whispered in commanding tones for she did not want to waken her dad who would be very cross if he was disturbed. He had to be up early so he would not be too pleased to be woken up at two o'clock in the morning.

Sarah rubbed Bingo down with a warm, dry towel, then quickly wiped the floor and hung the cloth on a chair. Giving the dog a biscuit, she hurried back to her bedroom. Looking out of her window, she felt sorry for anyone out on a night like this.

*   *   *

The dolphin swam into the shallow water towards the beach. 'This is as far as I can go,' it said to the boy on its back. 'It's a short swim from here. You belong on land, but be careful!'

The boy could hear the roar of the surf and the pounding of the waves on the rocks jutting out on either side of the cove. He hugged the dolphin and placed a kiss near its eye. Then he slid down from the dolphin's back and began to swim rapidly towards the shore, turning back briefly to the dolphin which seemed to nod reverently to him, before turning out to sea and diving beneath the waves.

The boy felt a tinge of loneliness as he waved goodbye to his enchanting companion. It was not long before he reached the beach. The rain lashed his body. He was chilled to the bone.

Beyond the beach he could see a wood. He knew he would find shelter there so, without delay, he ran towards the trees, leaping over a mound of tangled driftwood.

Clambering over a fence by the wood, he caught his right leg on some barbed wire. The sharp point tore deeply into his flesh. He winced with pain and put his hand on the wound to stem the flow of blood.

The wood looked menacing in the dark. The wind whistled through the trees and the rain continued to pour down. Picking up several branches, he made a cover for himself beside an oak tree. There he huddled down, waiting for the storm to abate.

Chapter 2

Sarah woke to find the sun pouring through the window and across the room. She stretched in the warm cosiness of her bed and rubbed the sleep from her eyes. Sitting up, she listened to the sounds of the morning. A song-thrush sang near her window, then immediately repeated his melody. A wren answered from the garden wall, before hopping down under a fuchsia shrub.

Sarah could hear her Gran bustling about the kitchen. Then the roar of the tractor sounded out in the fields. Sarah looked out the window to see how far away her father was. He was busy ploughing in the middle-distance. Dozens of screaming black-headed gulls followed the plough, ready to swoop down on the many insects disturbed when the earth was turned over.

Sarah glanced towards the wood where she had seen the strange light last night, but all she could see were some rooks were flying over the trees.

15

'Sarah! Sarah!'

'Coming, Gran,' she called. She dressed quickly and hurried to the bathroom for a quick wash before scrubbing her teeth and then racing down the stairs.

'Your Dad will be in for his breakfast any minute. Get me some eggs and rashers from the fridge. And take the hair out of your eyes. You'll get cross-eyes.'

Sarah flicked her fair hair back with her left hand.

'Be careful you don't get any hairs on the table,' warned Gran. 'Young girls nowadays …! In my day, our mothers would spend half-an-hour just brushing our hair.'

Then, realising what she had said, Gran sat down sadly. A tear ran from her left eye. Lifting up her apron, she wiped her cheek. Sarah hugged her.

'It's all right, Gran. I know Mum is in heaven watching over us.'

Gran smiled as more tears welled up in her eyes. 'Maybe she's having her hair brushed by Great-Gran!'

They hugged each other again. Suddenly, the door opened and Sarah's father came in, stopping beside the table.

'What's this then? Turtle-doves is it in my kitchen?' Sarah and her Gran stood away from each other. 'Where's my breakfast? I'm famished.'

Sarah rushed to put the pan on the cooker. Her father took off his hat and sat down.

'That's great! Breakfast not even ready and me with half a day's work done!'

'Oh, don't be giving out. Have a mug of tea – it will be ready in a minute,' Gran insisted.

'Put on the radio. I want to hear the weather forecast. Sarah, let Gran finish that. You get Mary and Jamie up. I don't want them late for school.'

'Right, Dad,' replied Sarah in a happy tone and hurried up the stairs.

Bill Robinson found it difficult to look at his elder daughter without thinking of his dead wife. Sarah was the image of her mother. And the scar across her eye was a constant reminder of that dreadful night.

He never spoke about it but Gran knew he blamed himself for the accident, even though the other driver had been charged with manslaughter. Not that it meant anything – he had got off scot-free. And her son had lost a wife and nearly a daughter.

He had become bitter and disillusioned. There was very little laughter in the house. Even his children did not bring him much pleasure – he would not let them. It was as if he did not want anyone to get too close to him again. He had few friends. He kept to himself, losing himself in his work.

Almost the only person he spoke to was Joe, his farm-hand, who was a bit sly and never had much to say anyway. He did not do too much work either for he had been on the farm for twenty years and the two men were used to one another.

Gran did not like Joe, knowing he was a bit of a character. The children didn't like him either, especially because he

17

sometimes teased them in a malicious sort of way.

Gran put her son's breakfast on the table and cut him some of the wholemeal bread she had baked earlier. She tried to be mother and companion to her son now that poor Janie was no longer there.

'More bloody storms tonight,' Bill said gruffly, as he swallowed a mouthful of fried egg. 'The fence Joe put up the other week along the edge of the wood is completely blown down after last night's winds.'

'I thought the roof was going to come off,' Gran answered. 'The whole pattern of the weather is changing. I'm sure of it. Maybe it's something to do with those forests they're cutting down – where is it, Argentina or Brazil or somewhere?'

'Ah, don't you be worrying about some foreign forests. Haven't we enough to be worrying about in our own country?'

'Still,' said Gran, 'I saw a very good programme on television the other evening. I think it was RTE or was it the BBC? One of them anyway ...'

'Buzz off,' Jamie suddenly yelled from upstairs.

'What's going on up there?' called Gran.

'Jamie won't get out of bed. He says he's not going to school.'

'Jamie, you're to get dressed right away or I'll deal with you myself, do you hear me?' Gran said firmly.

There was another yell from Jamie. His father started up the stairs. 'I want you three down here in two minutes, dressed and sitting at the table. Do I make myself clear?'

'Yes, Dad,' the three children answered in chorus.

'They're staying up too late, that's the problem. And they're taught no discipline anymore,' he grumbled. 'Well, I'd better be off. See you later.'

Putting on his hat, he noticed Jamie's shoes outside the door. He picked up one of them and felt the inside, which was very wet.

'Bloody hell! They've been left out all night. Do these kids think money grows on trees? They're new shoes, too.'

'I'll speak to them,' Gran interrupted as she handed him a scarf. He wrapped it round his neck.

'I wish you would,' he answered, walking out.

Gran looked at the kitchen floor and saw huge boot prints all over it. She sighed and muttered to herself: 'Sarah will have to wash that floor again today.'

Jamie slid down the banisters, knocking off some coats hanging on the newel post.

'Be careful!' shouted Gran.

'Is Dad gone?'

'Of course. He can't hang around all morning waiting for you lot to get up.' Mary hurried down the stairs, followed by Sarah.

During breakfast Sarah told the others about the light she had seen in the wood during the night.

'Probably someone out after rabbits or foxes.'

'I don't think so, Gran. It was definitely a light, sort of bluey-white.'

'Might have been a torch,' Gran said. 'One would want to be crazy to be out last night in the wood. Finish up your breakfasts and I'll make some lunch for you.'

As Sarah, Mary and Jamie walked to school half-a-mile away, they passed along by the wood. There were two fields between it and the road. Sarah stopped at the fence and stared across at the trees. She got a strange feeling.

'What's the matter?' asked Mary.

'I don't know,' Sarah wondered aloud, as if to herself.

'Come on,' said Mary. 'We don't want to be late.'

'No, you're right. Let's go.'

The three held hands and ran along the road, Jamie in the middle laughing loudly and trying to keep up with them. There were several children up ahead. As they passed them, the school bell rang out. Sarah went through the gate, then turned and gazed back in the direction from which they had come.

'Come on,' cried Mary. 'We'll be late.'

Sarah could not understand why she had become so obsessed with the wood. She certainly loved it; it was her secret place. She often sneaked out there at dusk to hear the long-eared owls hooting from the conifers. Sometimes she saw a badger or a fox. She knew nearly all the animals living there. But that light was so unusual.

During the morning, her mind kept turning back to it as she tried to puzzle out what it might have been. Could she have imagined it? Ms Palmer, her teacher, had scolded her twice for gazing out the window.

'Sarah Robinson, can you please tell me what's so important out there that you insist on looking for it?'

All eyes stared at Sarah. 'Oh, nothing, Ms Palmer.'

'That's three times I caught you gawking out the window.' The word brought a ripple of laughter from the class. 'Quiet! or I will give the whole class a hundred lines to write out. Have you been staying up late, Sarah? Is that why you are finding it difficult to concentrate?'

'Oh, no. It's just the storm last night … it … well, it scared me a little.'

'Yes, it was rather a bad one. Two of the slates came off my own roof during the night.' This brought muffled sniggers from some of the class. 'Now, that's enough about the storm. Just try to pay more attention, Sarah. Now, where was I? Oh, yes. In what year did Oliver Cromwell arrive in Ireland?'

After school, Sarah walked home with her friends, Betty and Gillian. Mary and Jamie had been collected earlier by Mrs Kennedy, who owned the bakery. Her son, who was in the same class as Jamie, was having a birthday party and Jamie and Mary had been invited.

Sarah glanced over her shoulder and then spoke to her friends in a hushed voice as if she was telling them a great secret. 'I saw something very strange last night in the wood.'

'What were you doing in the wood in the middle of the night?' asked Betty.

'I wasn't in the wood. I saw it from my bedroom window.'

'Let her tell us,' urged Gillian.

'Well, it was all dark in the wood but suddenly I saw a brilliant light. I'm sure it wasn't a torch, it was far too bright.'

'Maybe it was some kind of optical illusion,' suggested Betty.

'Maybe,' said Sarah doubtfully, 'but I can't imagine what.'

'It sounds like Spookland to me,' said Gillian.

'Well, I wasn't frightened at all. I was just curious. I still am. In fact, I think I will investigate the woods later on. Would you like to come?'

'Well, as long as it's not at night-time. Actually, no, I can't. I just remembered I have piano at half-past four. How about you, Gillian?'

'Well, sure … but …' Then she added, 'I think I might have to babysit for a while this afternoon.'

'Well, I'm going to find out, even if I have to go on my own.'

'If you see anything, be sure to tell us first. Promise?' Betty insisted.

'Of course I will. You two are my closest friends.' Then they parted.

'Good luck,' shouted Gillian, 'but be careful.'

'I will,' Sarah shouted back.

'Don't forget your promise to tell us first,' Betty added.

'Don't worry.'

*   *   *

'It sounds very exciting what Sarah saw, don't you think,' said Gillian, as she and Betty walked on together.

'Well, I don't know,' Betty answered somewhat doubtfully. 'You know that Sarah exaggerates a bit sometimes. Remember the time when she said she saw a wildcat in the wood and we all believed her because she knows so much about wildlife? It would have been the first time a wildcat was seen in Ireland and she thought it would be reported in the papers and everything. Remember?'

'Well, it *was* a cat,' said Gillian.

'Oh, yes, but just an *ordinary* cat that had been abandoned.'

'It did look like a wildcat,' insisted Gillian.

'Only to us who knew no better,' said Betty. 'Remember when Con Hughes, the librarian, investigated it and he's an expert on birds and things. He said it definitely was *not* a wildcat. He even thought we were trying to play a trick on him and didn't speak to us for weeks afterwards.'

'Yes,' replied Gillian. 'I remember it only too well. Still, it was fun to see old Hughes out with his camera, binoculars and net hoping to catch it. I think he expected to get his photograph in the papers.'

They both laughed loudly, remembering the incident.

*   *   *

Sarah hurried home and peered through the back window. She could see Gran sleeping in the big chair. Lifting the latch gently so as not to waken her, she tiptoed upstairs. Every step seems to creak when you want to go quietly, she thought to herself.

Quickly she changed out of her uniform and hurried downstairs, checked that her Gran was still asleep and pulled on her wellies to head out to the wood. She was half-way out the door again when Gran woke with a start and called out: 'Sarah, where are you off to?'

'Oh, just out for a walk with Bingo,' replied Sarah, edging out of the door a bit further and dreading the next question.

'Have you done your homework?'

'Not yet, Gran, but we don't have very much. It won't take me long.'

'And what about the potatoes for the dinner? Are you going to leave everything to your poor old Gran?'

Sarah felt guilty now about sneaking off. After all, Gran was eighty last birthday.

'All right, Gran,' she said, resigning herself to the inevitable. She took off her wellies again and started up the stairs, grabbing a slice of bread off the table as she passed. Stuffing it into her mouth, she began her homework.

Geography! It's so boring, she thought. 'When I'm older,' she said to herself, 'I'll just buy a map. Simple! Well, I'd better get it out of the way so I can start on the potatoes.'

*　　　*　　　*

Sarah did not manage to get to the wood until the evening when Gran was watching 'Coronation Street' and her Dad was snoring in his chair with the evening paper wide open on his lap. Putting on her heavy coat and the wellies, she opened the door. On the way out she felt a tug at her coat.

'Where are you going?' asked Jamie.

'Just for a short walk with the dog. He needs the exercise.'

'Can I come too?'

'No,' replied Sarah. 'Seven-year-old little boys should be in bed by now.'

'I'm nearly eight,' replied Jamie. 'I'm going to ask Daddy.'

'Don't you dare wake Dad up. He's having a rest after his dinner.'

'I want to come. Why can't I?' insisted the boy.

'Listen, if you stay here and be quiet I'll bring you back a surprise.'

'What will it be?' asked Jamie.

'A surprise. It wouldn't be a surprise if I told you, now would it?'

*　　　*　　　*

Sarah looked across the field. 'Here, Bingo. Come on, boy.'

The collie came bounding over and jumped up on her.

'Down, boy.'

She wiped the marks of his muddy paws from her coat. The dog ran a few yards, then quickly circled Sarah and ran a little farther, sniffing parts of the field for rabbit scent.

'Where are you off to, Missie?' shouted Joe, who was leaning on a fence.

'Oh, you startled me, Joe. I'm just going for a walk.'

'Don't lie around in the fields. I might mistake you for a rabbit. I'd hate to waste a cartridge on you.' He laughed loudly.

'Anyone ever tell you it's cruel to shoot wild creatures?'

'You have, many a time. It hasn't stopped me yet though,' he said, laughing even louder. She looked at him contemptuously.

'There's more feeling in a wet rag than in your entire body.'

'Is that so, Missie? Well, let me tell you, when I see any of your furry friends around here I look forward to plugging them.'

'Come on, Bingo,' Sarah called to the dog. 'Let's get out of here.' Laughing uproariously, Joe lit up a cigarette.

*   *   *

Black clouds passed overhead, revealing a silvery moon. Sarah could see the beach from the top of the hill. It seemed to be bathed in an eerie glow. On she went till she reached the edge of the wood. The trees looked different in the dark – bigger and more frightening. Shadows lay everywhere.

As she moved deeper into the wood, she trod on a twig. The sharp crack made her jump. She couldn't understand why. She had often before been to the wood in the evening and felt no fear.

Then she stopped in her tracks. Up ahead she thought she saw the bright light again, fainter than last night but just the same. Swallowing fast, she caught Bingo by the collar and moved on. A woodcock fluttered past with a cry of alarm, which gave her a fright. She looked behind and could see the silvery moonlight beyond the edge of the wood.

On she moved, wishing she had brought the torch. She sensed that someone was watching her and she looked all round several times, her eyes adjusting somewhat to the dark.

Then she felt some strange drops of rain and the branches of the surrounding trees began to rustle. The weather forecast had promised another storm. She decided to turn back. As she did, Bingo ran ahead. 'Bingo, Bingo, come back, Bingo!' She hurried after him, the twigs cracking under her feet as she moved. Then she stopped suddenly. A few yards away he stood, almost luminous in the dark – a beautiful-looking boy with golden curls cascading down his face. His eyes were like pools of blue. He looked fragile, standing there in his nakedness. She had never seen a more beautiful person.

She wanted to say something but couldn't find her voice. She stood transfixed, watching this strange boy whose form seemed to glow against the dark background. They stared at each other, eyes wide and unblinking. Awestruck, she reached out slowly with her right hand, her fingers tingling.

She closed both eyes tightly, then slowly opened one. He was still there. She leaned forward and touched his face to see if he was real or an illusion and felt his soft, white skin. Filled with excitement, she finally plucked up the courage to speak. Her mouth was open before the sound came out.

'Who … who are you? What is your name?'

A puzzled look came over the boy's face. Then she asked him again 'What is your name?'

The boy's mind worked quickly, adjusting to the language that was being spoken to him. He answered softly. 'My name is …' He paused for a moment, then sang a most beautiful phrase. Sarah was dumbstruck.

'What a beautiful sound!' she exclaimed. 'I've never heard anything so wonderful.' Then she added, slightly puzzled: 'Is that really your name?'

'Yes,' he replied warmly.

'Where have you come from and what are you doing here in our wood?'

'It is difficult to explain where I come from. All I know is that I wanted to come here and see for myself.'

'See what?' asked Sarah.

'Everything. To make connections. To try to understand, to experience, to share.'

'You know, all this sounds very weird,' said Sarah. 'I wonder is this some dream I'm going to awaken from in the morning.' The rain began to fall heavily.

'Oh, heavens, what time is it? I must be going. My Dad usually goes out at night for a pint. He will kill me if he finds me out wandering in the wood at this hour. I must find my dog, though he's probably chasing rabbits. Sorry, I must go.'

She started to run back home. Then she turned round and said: 'Oh, good night. Can we meet again tomorrow? Here in the wood at three o'clock. Is that okay?'

'Yes,' the boy answered.

'Great,' she replied, then added gently, 'my name is Sarah. Sarah Robinson … Bye.'

Sarah hurried to the edge of the wood. The clouds were darkening and the rain was falling quite heavily now as she ran down the hill, pulling her coat over her head. Bingo suddenly ran straight across her, almost making her trip.

'You silly mutt. Come on, let's get home. Fast!'

She could see the lights of the kitchen and sitting-room. Hoping her Dad had not gone out or she would be in big trouble, she arrived at the back door. The dog started to bark.

'Quiet, Bingo.'

Lifting the latch, she peered round the door. No-one in the kitchen. Quickly she pulled off her coat and wellies and crept upstairs. As she reached her bedroom, her sister Mary came in.

'How come you're not in bed?' she asked.

'I'm just going,' replied Sarah sharply. 'Nine-year-olds like you should be asleep by now.'

'I don't like the thunder, it scares me,' Mary replied, and Sarah felt sorry for snapping at her.

'Listen, why don't you take Brownie into your bed. He'll be nice to cuddle.'

'Can I really?' Mary asked excitedly.

'Of course, you can.' The teddy-bear was Sarah's favourite soft toy. Her Uncle Pat had sent it from America for her fourth birthday. She had often cried herself to sleep clutching it after her Mum had died.

A roll of thunder boomed and Mary gripped Sarah in fright.

'It's okay. Brownie will mind you.'

They could hear their Dad downstairs. 'Don't wait up for me,' he was saying. 'I'm just popping down for a quick one. If Joe calls, tell him I'm gone down.'

'Right you be. Be careful on the roads,' Gran warned.

'I will. Sarah, are you in bed yet?'

'Nearly, Dad.'

'Well, hurry along in and put out the light. That girl, she never stops reading – just like her mother. They'd both read all night if you'd let them.'

'Ah, it does her no harm. Broadens the mind,' said Gran. 'I'm only sorry I didn't read more myself when I was her age. Now, be off with you. It's another miserable night. I wouldn't go out in it myself for all the tea in China.'

'And you who loves tea,' added Bill with a half-smile.

'Will you get out with yourself.' Gran locked the back door. Then she opened it again. 'Have you got the front-door key?'

'Yes', shouted Bill as he got into his car.

*   *   *

Sarah sat on the edge of the bed in the dark, waiting for the car to pull out. When she was sure it had left the front yard, she hurried to the window and looked out into the bleak night. Poor fellow out there in the wood all alone, getting soaked to the skin, she thought, and him without a stitch of clothes to wear. Where did he come from and would he be all right? Maybe he's an orphan, she thought.

He must have gone for a swim and lost his clothes! There was something very different about him. He looked so pale and fragile. The more she thought about him, the more she felt she must do something.

She quickly got dressed again and sneaked down the stairs, putting on her boots and wrapping herself up well. Gently she pulled over the bolt, lifted the latch and went out into the night.

The wind was still raging and the rain beat down, making it difficult to see. She was soaked already. She headed up the fields to the wood, hoping she would find him. Then she saw a faint glow and hurried towards it. She saw him crouched under some branches.

'Hi again! Look, it's a terrible night and I don't think

you should stay out in the wood. Come down with me to the barn and you can sleep in the hayloft. I'm sorry I can't bring you into the house. It would take too much explaining. Please come, you will be warm and dry down there.'

'Thank you, Sarah. You have a kind heart.'

Sarah felt a bit embarrassed at his kind comment. 'Oh, I wouldn't leave a dog out on a night like this.' Then she realised this was not the right thing to say. 'Of course, I don't mean to suggest you're a dog or anything,' she hurried on. 'What I meant was ...'

'I know very well what you meant, Sarah,' he assured her. 'Just lead the way and I will follow.'

*   *   *

Down they ran towards the farm, the rain making it hard to see the way. Finally they reached the gate, closed it quietly behind them and raced to the barn.

'Whew! What a night. You will be safe and dry here. Make a bed on the hay over there and here are some sacks you can use as blankets. I'll have to be getting back home. I'll try to get you some food early in the morning and some ...' she paused, then gestured, ... 'clothes. You can't be going round like that. The local sergeant will arrest you! I'll find some old clothes to fit you. You're about twelve or thirteen, right?'

'Right,' he replied.

'Well, which?'

'Twelve earthly years is correct.'

'You *are* very strange, if you don't mind me saying so. "Twelve earthly years". I've never heard anyone's age described like that before. Anyway, I'll go now. Make sure to stay under cover and don't let Dad or Joe, our farm-hand, see you. Hope you'll be okay.'

'Thank you, Sarah,' he assured her. 'I'll be fine.'

'Until the morning, then,' she replied. 'Sleep well.'

Sarah gave him a quick kiss on the cheek. She pulled back in amazement for his skin smelled like wild flowers. Then, looking down, she saw the deep gash on his leg.

'Oh, you poor boy. That's a deep cut. I'll bring a plaster and some ointment for it in the morning.'

'Don't trouble yourself. Yet it is very strange how pain courses through a human body.'

'Yes,' she replied, looking puzzled. Then, remembering an abscess on her mouth after being struck by a hockey ball, she added: 'Wait till you get a toothache – then you'll know all about pain. Now I must really go.'

She hurried away and ran to the kitchen door. 'Oh, no! It's locked!' she winced. 'Gran must have locked it and gone to bed. What will I do?'

She checked the windows but they were all bolted. Luckily her father had not yet returned but she could not wait until he arrived or he would be very angry.

In desperation, she started to throw pebbles at her sister's bedroom window. 'Mary, Mary, open the door,' she called. Mary awoke after several pebbles hit the glass but ducked back immediately under the blankets.

'Mary ... Mary.'

She could hear her name being called. Finally plucking up courage to investigate, she pressed her face against the window. Craning her neck to look down, she saw Sarah waving frantically, making wild gestures.

Mary hurried down the stairs and quickly unbolted the door.

'Ah, you're all sopping wet ...'

'Sshhh!' whispered Sarah, 'we don't want to waken Gran.'

Suddenly they heard the noise of a car and the headlights swept round into the farmyard. 'Quick, it's Dad. Let's get up to bed.'

'What were you up to anyway?' asked Mary.

'Never mind that now. I'll tell you tomorrow. But it's a great secret and you must keep it to yourself. Promise, cross your heart!'

'I promise.'

They climbed quietly up the landing. Downstairs they could hear their father and Joe talking about the match they had watched on TV in the pub. Sarah tucked Mary in with Brownie. 'Goodnight. God bless!'

'God bless you too, Sarah. And don't forget to tell me your secret.'

'I promise.'

'Who's walking around up there?' her father called from the bottom of the stairs.

'It's only me, Dad, going to the toilet.'

'Okay. Goodnight, Sarah.'

'Night, Dad.'

Sarah lay on her bed, going over all the things that had happened. She wondered where the boy had come from and why it sounded like music when he spoke his name. She thought about the peck on the cheek she had given him and his skin smelling of wild flowers. That must have been because he had been in the wood.

His face was so calm and serene. Had he run away from home? Maybe he was a visitor from outer space?

This is crazy, she argued in her mind. Well, whatever he is, he is a very gentle person and he needs help. The drumming of the rain was momentarily drowned out by a crash of thunder. Then she whispered to the night: 'Sleep well, my special friend ...'

Slowly she drifted into a peaceful slumber.

Chapter 3

Peering over the blankets, Sarah could see the beautiful sunshine streaming in the window. It had been raining steadily all night so it was a refreshing change to see clear blue skies and to hear the birds singing. There were more of them than usual, she thought to herself, as she saw them sitting on the barn roof singing their hearts out.

She got dressed quickly, putting on her uniform until she remembered it was Saturday morning. Then she slipped into jeans and a heavy blue sweater and hurried downstairs. All the others were having breakfast, including her father who was reading last night's newspaper. Sarah bounded in.

'Good morning, Dad, Gran, Mary and dear brother Jamie!'

'You're a bright spark this morning, Sarah. What's up with you?'

'Nothing, Gran. It's such a lovely day I feel wonderful and hungry'.

'What's new about feeling hungry?' added her father, looking over his paper.

Slipping a napkin from the kitchen drawer, Sarah picked two thick slices of brown bread, lightly buttering them and then spreading raspberry jam plentifully on top.

Using one hand, she lifted the cereal and shook it into a bowl. With her other hand, she placed the napkin on her knee and put the bread into it. Then she reached for an apple and a banana.

'Now, don't be greedy, Sarah,' said Gran. 'Take one or the other.' Sarah replaced the apple on the table.

* * *

When breakfast was over and everyone had left the kitchen, Sarah took some tea-cake and the apple, then got orange juice from the fridge. As she closed the fridge door, she noticed Joe who was walking towards the barn.

'Oh, Joe,' she called, rushing outside.

'Yes, Missie,' he replied. 'To what do I owe the pleasure of this visit? I hope you're not going to start on about your little furry friends.'

'Well, no.' Sarah was desperately trying to think of a way to distract him from the barn.

'You know that fat pheasant you've been chasing? Well, I heard him this morning ... I think he is in ... the meadow!'

'Really?' said Tom excitedly. Then he got suspicious.

'How come you're sharing this little bit of information with me about one of your feathered friends?'

'Well, I was hoping you might make me a bird-box for the garden and maybe the blue tits would nest in it next spring ...'

'Do you think I have nothing better to do than building little nest boxes for your dicky birds. Why can't they build nests for themselves like the rest of the birds?'

'But I thought ...'

'See what thought did!' said Joe, rudely interrupting her. 'But thanks for telling me. I'll just go and get my shotgun.'

'You're just mean,' said Sarah.

'And you're a smart little Missie. But you need to be up very early to outsmart me!' He hurried off, sniggering to himself.

Sarah had known all along he would be distracted by her story about the pheasant and that he would spend half the morning looking for it.

Rushing back to the kitchen, she grabbed the food and headed towards the barn only to be confronted by Mary and Jamie who were hiding behind the barn door.

'What's the big secret?' Jamie demanded.

Sarah turned angrily to Mary. 'Why did you have to go and tell him about the secret?'

'Well, why not?' she answered. 'He told me plenty of secrets about the hedgehog and the frog.'

'This is different,' said Sarah. 'Listen. I'm going to let you meet someone. He is a very special boy. He has no home and he needs our help but I don't want Dad, Gran or Joe to know about him yet, okay?'

'Okay,' they agreed together.

'Cross your hearts.' They did as they were told. Then Sarah led them inside.

There they found Bingo sitting across the boy's lap and lots of birds perched on the bales of hay. Among them were a song-thrush, a blackbird, a robin, a linnet, a bullfinch, a chaffinch and a wood-pigeon. The birds scattered when the children entered.

'Wow!' said Jamie, 'look at all those birds.'

'Good morning,' Sarah said to the boy. 'Did you sleep all right?' The boy nodded.

'I brought you some breakfast. Oh, this is my sister, Mary ... say hello, Mary.'

'Hello,' said Mary, 'and this is Jamie, our brother.'

'Why don't you have any clothes on?' Jamie asked.

'Don't be rude,' said Sarah, a little embarrassed.

'He's being rude without any clothes on.'

'Yes, I must get some clothes,' said the boy.

'I have some clothes that will fit you,' said Sarah. 'I'll be back in a jiffy.' She hurried out of the barn.

Mary and Jamie stared at the boy.

'Eat your breakfast,' said Jamie.

'Thank you, I will.'

The boy closed his eyes and whispered something like a blessing over the food. Then he began to eat slowly.

'It's good, isn't it?' said Mary. 'Gran made the bread.'

'The jam was bought in the shop,' said Jamie, then he asked the boy what age he was and what was his name. The boy replied that he was twelve and then spoke his name. As he did, all the birds broke into song.

'That was beautiful,' said Mary.' 'How did you do that?'

'Is that really your name?' said Jamie. 'What kind of name is that? No-one will be able to say it but you.'

Just then, Sarah returned with a red check shirt, blue denim jeans and black runners.

'Here you are. These should fit you. They're a bit worn but they're clean.'

'Thank you, Sarah. You are very thoughtful.'

'You can dress behind the bales of hay,' she suggested.

As the boy jumped down, Sarah noticed that the wound in his leg had completely healed. How curious, she thought, but said nothing. Then he stood up and showed himself in his new clothes.

'Is this all right?' he asked.

'Fine,' said Sarah. 'When you're finished your breakfast, we'll go for a walk.'

'I want to come too,' said Jamie.

'So do I,' added Mary.

* * *

The village, with the harbour at its heart, looked very pretty in the morning sunshine. The four children strolled towards the pier. Sarah stopped suddenly, anxiety showing in her face.

'What's the matter?' asked Mary.

'Well, if any of our friends meet us, they will want to meet you and to know your name,' she said to the boy. 'We know your name sounds lovely but we wouldn't be able to say it.'

'Well, you can call me after my other friend if you like,' replied the boy.

'What's that?'

'Dolphin,' he answered. This brought hoots of laughter from the other children. The boy looked surprised.

'Sorry,' Sarah said, trying to stifle a laugh, 'but my friends would find that just as funny as we did. No, we'll just have to think of something better.'

'How about Bird?' suggested Jamie. 'After all, they all seemed to like him.'

'That's very good,' Sarah said. 'Maybe it would be better as a surname. We're called Robinson,' she explained to be boy. 'Now you will be called Bird.'

'I understand,' he said.

'Good,' added Sarah. 'Now what will we use as a Christian name? I think it should be something from nature, something that would suit your free spirit. Oh yes, I've got it ... Rowan! It's the name of a tree and it's also used sometimes as a boy's name,' she exclaimed with delight.

'That sounds fine to me,' the boy smiled.

Sarah stopped again, then looking slightly embarrassed she turned to the boy. 'Look, Rowan. I think perhaps it

41

would be better if we didn't go to the village just yet. Let's go to the wood – it's my secret place.'

'Yea,' agreed Jamie. 'Okay, Rowan?'

The boy nodded his head and his long curls fell across his eyes. Then, with a stroke from his hand, he pushed his hair back out of the way.

As they walked across the gravel towards the fields, the boy noticed a worm trying to move over the small pebbles. Stooping down, he gently picked it up.

'Poor little worm, you will dry out before you reach the grass.' Then the boy walked over to the edge of the field and placed the worm down carefully. Sarah glanced at Mary and Jamie. Then Mary opened the gate.

'I want to climb over it,' said Jamie, annoyed at being deprived of his little pleasure.

'Well, the gate is open now,' replied Mary with authority, 'so just come on.'

Sarah, Mary and Rowan moved into the field. 'Come on,' called Sarah to Jamie who stood where he was, kicking at the gravel. Then he closed the gate in front of him and climbed over it.

On they walked through the bright morning. Leaves were falling softly from the great chestnut trees which had been ablaze with autumnal colours a few weeks before. A bird flew up from the ground.

'Look', called Sarah excitedly, 'a jay.'

'It's lovely,' replied the boy.

Mary asked if it was a rare bird.

'Yes,' said Sarah. 'Well, no ... not rare ...' She hesitated, not wishing to make a mistake in front of Rowan. Then she added more confidently: 'Actually, it's rarely seen because it's a shy bird. It's a member of the crow family.'

'It doesn't look like a crow,' said Jamie.

'Well, it is anyhow,' she replied.

Just then, Bingo arrived and began to run round them. He gave a gentle bark and Sarah bent down to greet him. 'Hi, fella, where were you? I hope you weren't chasing the rabbits.' She tossed his ears and the dog bounded around her playfully.

Jamie stood beside the chestnut tree and threw up a stick to knock down a nut. Every throw fell short of even the lowest branch.

'What's Jamie doing?' the boy asked.

'Oh, he's trying to knock down a conker from the tree.' said Sarah. 'You have heard of conkers, haven't you? It's a game boys play,' and she explained it to him.

Then she called to Jamie. 'Come on,' she said. 'There are plenty on the ground if you just look for them.'

'But I want that one,' he insisted, pointing to a fat, prickly seed-case on a high branch at the side of the tree.

'May I try?' asked the boy.

'Well, of course,' said Sarah, a little surprised.

Jamie handed Rowan the stick and pointed up to the tree. 'See that one there. It's way up; can you see it?'

The boy took the stick and paused for a moment, staring hard at the precise spot. Then with a sudden swing of his arm he catapulted the piece of wood into the air. They all watched as it curved and twisted its way to the target.

'Wow,' Jamie yelled delightedly. 'That was a deadly shot.'

He ran quickly to collect his prize and burst open the cracked husk to reveal the shiny brown nut.

They all ran over to join him.

'See,' he said proudly. 'I told you it would be a good one.'

They all laughed and moved on towards the wood.

Mary broke into song. 'There was a farmer had a dog and Bingo was his name-o ...'

Jamie joined in, followed by Sarah. Then the boy took up the song with them and the dog barked.

Across the water-logged ploughed field walked Joe, a shotgun in one hand and a dead rabbit held by the ears in the other. He stopped when he saw the children.

'There's little Missie,' he growled, 'sending me on a wild goose chase for the cock pheasant. Still, I'll let her know that I managed to plug one of her furry friends.'

The wood was filled with November's uncertain light. A gentle serenity filled the place, as if it was hallowed ground.

Sarah looked around. The wood seemed more special today than ever. How things can change, she thought, remembering the storm when the wood was a frightening place and the trees took on sinister forms.

'Would you like me to show you some of the wood's secrets?' she asked the boy, looking into his crystal eyes.

'Yes,' Jamie piped up.

'So would I,' Mary added.

'Come this way,' said Sarah in hushed tones. They tiptoed through the wood.

'What are we going to see?' Jamie asked loudly.

'We're supposed to be quiet,' shushed Mary .

'Well, why are you talking?' argued Jamie.

'There,' Sarah pointed confidently.

Jamie screwed up his face. 'You mean that broken part of the tree?'

Sarah nodded.

'What's so great about that?'

'It's a squirrel's drey,' she informed him.

Mary jumped up and down excitedly. 'Look! Look! A squirrel.'

They all looked up to see it move nervously and erratically through the branches. Then another could be seen clinging to the bark of a beech, before scurrying up into the branches.

'That was exciting,' said the boy.

'Yes,' agreed Sarah, 'and it was a red squirrel too, my favourite kind,' indicating that she was familiar with the two types of squirrel. 'Did you know that the grey squirrel comes from America and is not native to these parts?'

'No,' the boy said appreciatively.

She was about to explain more when she noticed he

was looking at her with a gentle penetrating stare and it made her a little uncomfortable.

She began to wonder if she was showing off her knowledge a little bit rather than gently sharing it with him. It was lovely to look into his eyes. Yet, she felt they had the power to see right into her mind. They were not frightening or critical, more like a light shining through the darkness.

'There is something over here, even more special,' she called.

They walked through a carpet of leaves to the top of a wide mound surrounded by beech trees. Pointing to a large entrance in the ground, she revealed another of her secrets.

'This is a badger sett and it's still in use. You can see the fresh clay and the clean entrance.'

'There's another hole over here,' called Jamie.

'And here,' added Mary.

'There are several entrances and the animals live below in the chambers,' Sarah explained.

'Will we see one?' asked Jamie.

'Not now, they are too shy and wary. Like most wild creatures, they are afraid of people. We might see one some evening. We could bring a torch. But we would have to keep very quiet.'

In another part of the wood, Bingo flushed a wood-cock, which flew up and startled them.

'Oh, isn't that beautiful?' said Sarah. 'I'd never seen a

woodcock before last night except in books or in a delicatessen, hanging from a hook.' She stopped. Somehow the thought of the dead bird seemed grotesque. She shouted after the woodcock: 'Good luck! I'm glad you escaped Joe's greedy eyes.'

Up ahead, stood a magnificent oak. Its spreading branches lay bare, letting in the delicate light.

'This is my favourite spot in the whole wood,' Sarah said, closing her eyes and stretching out her arms as if in praise. She was amazed how relaxed she felt with Rowan, as she had named him. Even though he was a complete stranger, it was as if she had known him all her life.

Normally, she would not hang around with boys. Most of the local youths were immature and a downright pain, always showing off or yanking her long fair hair. Rowan was different. She thought back on the previous night and wondered if it was all in her imagination – the light in the wood and everything. Yet there he was, sitting with Mary and Jamie and Bingo and wearing her old clothes.

He glanced over at her. 'This is really a wonderful place, Sarah. Thank you for showing it to me.'

Sarah was pleased. He had away of making a person feel special. She wanted to ask him all sorts of questions but did not want to appear inquisitive. Then, although she knew it was completely healed, she asked him about the gash in his leg.

'It's better, thank you,' he replied.

'Sarah had a terrible cut on her face but it's cured now,

except that you can still see the scar,' said Jamie.

Sarah pulled her long hair across her face as if to cover the mark. Then she fell silent, remembering that terrible night and the phone call with the news that her mother would never be home again. Tears welled up in her eyes.

Quickly she brushed both eyes with her sleeve. 'Listen,' she said to the others, 'we'll have to go now. Dad and Gran will be expecting us for lunch.' She turned to the boy: 'Sorry I can't invite you but I'll bring you something later. Will you be staying on here?'

'Yes,' he replied gently.

'Come on, Mary and Jamie. Let's go.'

Sarah paused, remembering her two friends, Betty and Gillian.

'Do you mind if I bring a couple of other girls to meet you this afternoon? They're my best friends.'

'That would be lovely. I'll look forward to seeing you all later.'

'Bye for now,' said Mary warmly.

'See you,' said Jamie.

Jamie winked. The boy winked back.

Then he called: 'Sarah!'

She walked back a few steps and stood beside him. He gazed steadily at her and she stared back, transfixed by the magnificent radiance of his blue eyes. It was like bathing in a calm, blue lake. A strange and beautiful peace spread through her mind. She seemed suspended in a wondrous dream, floating to the stars.

It was such a good feeling, like the feeling a baby has when it snuggles up to its mother, or a climber reaching the summit of a high mountain, or the fragrance of wild flowers or the touch of a gentle breeze on a warm day. It was all these things and more.

Then his gentle voice sounded in her head. 'It's better not to dwell on past hurts, for mental wounds can open much more easily than physical ones. Remember the happy times with your mother.'

A golden presence seemed to hover above her and a wonderful feeling of peace soaked through her.

Suddenly Sarah realised that she was staring at the boy. She couldn't remember how long she had stood there. It seemed an eternity, yet it could only have been a few minutes because Mary and Jamie were still only a little of the way home.

They parted in silence. Sarah gave a quick glance over her shoulder. He seemed to be kneeling down. Perhaps he is praying, she thought.

As they got near the house, Sarah asked the others what they thought of Rowan.

'I like him,' Mary answered directly.

'So do I,' said Jamie. 'But how come he was in our barn this morning?'

'Listen, we will have to keep him secret from the grown-ups for the moment and that includes Dad and Gran, okay?' Sarah insisted, holding their shoulders. Then she added: 'It's only till we find out a bit more about him.

Then we can tell them. Until then it will just be our little secret. Right?'

'Right,' they replied.

As they reached the gate, they were shocked to see a dead rabbit tied up by its ears on the hedge.

'Aah,' exclaimed Sarah, disgusted.

'That's cruel,' said Mary.

'Poor thing,' exclaimed Jamie.

Joe watched from behind a hedgerow with his hand over his mouth to stifle a laugh.

'It's that mean, cruel guttersnipe, Joe, who did this. I'm going to tell Dad,' Sarah raged.

Clicking the latch hard, they pushed into the kitchen. Their father sat eating as he watched the racing on the television.

'Dad, will you talk to Joe about the way he ...' Sarah began.

Before she could finish the sentence, her Dad swung round and shouted: 'Would you for goodness's sake come in a bit quietly? You nearly took the door off the hinges. And would the last one in please close that door. You would get your end sitting here. It's not the height of summer, you know.'

'Look at Jamie,' said Gran, 'his coat wide open and there's a chill in the air.'

The children kicked off their boots and sat down. Their father continued to look at the television.

'Dad,' said Sarah. 'Do you know what Joe McGuire did?

He killed a rabbit and he hung it up by the ears just to upset us.'

'Don't be bothering me now like a good girl. Can't you see I'm watching something?'

'Leave your father be,' said Gran, placing plates of food down in front of them. 'It's great service around here for people who are late for their dinner.'

'Lunch, Gran,' Mary said mildly.

'Don't get uppity with me, young lady, or it will be the wooden spoon for you. I'm warning you now!'

'She didn't mean it the way it sounded, Gran,' Sarah shot back, trying to smooth things out. 'You know Mary is always precise about things. She doesn't ever mean to hurt.'

'Well, it does hurt at times. Your own mother, Lord rest her soul, could be just as cutting.'

Bill Robinson threw his arms up in the air.

'Could I have a bit of hush in here? It's been a tough week for me. Besides,' he added in lighter tones, 'I have a bet on Red Fox.'

'Which one is he, Dad?' Jamie asked with interest.

'The one in the red and black colours.'

Chapter 4

An hour or so later, when Sarah, Mary and Jamie came out again from the house, they noticed several children, including Gillian and Betty, making their way along the hedgerow.

'Where are you all going?' Sarah asked angrily. Gillian confessed that she had told Mary Ryan and Eleanor Crosbie that 'someone special' was in the wood.

'It was supposed to be a secret I shared with you,' Sarah said sharply.

Then her sister owned up that she also had told her best friends, Helen and Justine.

'Oh, great,' said Sarah accusingly. 'We should have put up a sign and told the whole village. We'd better hurry before we're seen by Dad or that weasel, Joe. C'mon.'

Sarah caught up with the other children. 'What are you all doing here?' she asked.

Mary Ryan spoke first. 'We've come to see the young

fella who lives in the wood.'

'He's supposed to be very special or something,' added another.

'He's just an orphan who got shipwrecked and made his way into the wood, that's all,' said Sarah firmly. 'Now will you all please leave? My Dad doesn't want the whole village trampling through his fields.'

'Is he a pirate?' asked one small boy with glasses.

'Don't be stupid,' scolded his bigger brother.

'We're not leaving until we've seen him,' insisted one of the girls.

Sarah bit her lip. 'Okay, but you must be quiet. If we're stopped, tell whoever it is that we're on a nature walk, okay?'

And the band of twenty or so children with Sarah, Mary and Jamie in front moved into the next field.

Suddenly Joe appeared from behind the hedgerow. The children stopped in their tracks.

'Well, what's going on here, Missie?'

'If you must know, I'm taking my friends for a nature walk,' retorted Sarah.

'Oh, I see, Missie David Attenborough. Explaining all about the birds and bees and the little furry things with the long ears that are good to snare and finally to eat,' he said, pushing his face up to Sarah. His bad breath made her recoil.

'Have you never heard of toothpaste?'

Joe's face grimaced with temper. 'You little ...'

'What's all this, Sarah?' asked her father, stepping out

from the other side of the hedgerow.

'Oh, Dad! Just a little nature walk with some friends.'

Mr Robinson eyed the crowd of children suspiciously. 'You're sure it's nature and not some other bit of mischief?'

'Yes, Dad,' Sarah insisted.

'Well, be off, but no lighting fires or anything like that.'

'No, Dad.' They hurried off.

Joe shouted after them. 'Don't damage any of those fences that have taken me ages to repair!'

'Kids!' sighed Mr Robinson. 'Still, it's good to see them enjoying themselves. Then he turned to Joe. 'I don't want you upsetting them. I heard about the rabbit incident.'

Joe looked uncomfortable.

'Sorry, Bill, but you know there's a bit of the poacher in me veins. I suppose not having kids of my own I do forget how squeamish they are.'

Mr Robinson was unmoved. 'Come on,' he said. 'Let's collect on Red Fox – at twenty to one!' They walked away down the hill.

Sarah looked after them and saw them disappearing round a bend in the road.

'The coast is clear,' she said confidently to the others. 'Now listen. Before we meet Rowan, remember you are not in a zoo gawking at some poor creature behind the bars. I admit he is a special kind of boy. I don't know exactly how to explain it, but he is different and he might even be an orphan, so don't be rude or use any bad language.' They all nodded.

As they moved quietly through the wood, Sarah was becoming more and more anxious by the minute. Perhaps, she thought, she was creating some kind of mystery by her talk. Maybe he was just some runaway from a school or a place where young criminals were held. Was the whole thing something that would make a laughing-stock of her?

She was even half-hoping that Rowan wouldn't be in the wood at all and that she could simply forget the whole thing. Many of the children would be annoyed that they had come on a wild goose chase but her friends would forgive her.

As these thoughts chased round her mind, she suddenly saw him. He seemed to be kneeling, as when they had left him before going in for lunch.

By the time they reached the oak, he was sitting on a fallen log. They gathered round him in a circle, stopping and staring at him. He looks beautiful, thought Gillian. The others too seemed to be dazzled by his appearance.

The boy turned round and gazed at each one of them individually, his eyes seeming to look into their very hearts. Each one of them felt the same sense of joy, like when one is surprised by the arrival of a close friend one hasn't seem for a long time.

Jamie broke the silence by walking over to the boy.

'Meet Rowan,' said Sarah. 'Well, say hello ...'

Like a chorus they all repeated, 'Hello.'

'Sit down. There's no need to be afraid. He won't bite,'

urged Sarah. glancing at the boy. He smiled back.

Jamie pulled some sweets from his pocket and gave the boy one. Most of the other children seemed to have the same idea. One after another, they produced chocolate, crisps and sweets to offer him. This brought a broad smile to the boy's face and they all laughed with him.

After a while, when they had shared and eaten the sweets, Gillian asked the boy if he had any family. The other children suddenly stopped their chattering to hear his answer.

He spoke quietly. 'Oh, yes, I have a family, a very big family. I consider all of you to be my family.'

This seemed to please them. Then he continued: 'I made this journey here on my own. I wanted to get a closer look at this world, to share, to learn and to understand more. We are all discovering new things every day, every moment, and we can use these ideas in a creative and caring way.'

The children looked at one another, a little puzzled at his words. Then he went on: 'When an artist, a poet or a composer makes something new, they are adding to creation, for us to share and enjoy. We can all be artists, using kindness and caring to create new joys and new wonders. In this way, the world and all its people will be made richer and become more fully human. In time, this will lead to even greater wonders not yet even dreamt of.'

The children were silent for a little time. Then Gillian spoke up and asked if these ideas could work in friendships.

'To achieve a beautiful friendship with another human person is to begin the process of realising perfection,' he said.

As he went on speaking, Sarah was nearly dumbstruck by the conversation. She could hardly believe that Gillian, who normally spoke only about films or fashion, and the others who were interested mainly in things like football and the latest pop songs, could be listening so intently to what the boy was saying.

They continued to talk and share ideas with the boy but mainly they wanted just to listen to him and to be with him.

Sarah herself wanted to know more and to understand some of the things he had said, but she felt she could do this only when they were alone.

The darkness was beginning to creep into the sky, yet it was only late afternoon. She suggested that it was time for them to leave and that they should all go home for tea. Reluctantly, they began to walk away but not before extending a hand for the boy to shake. Each of them felt an inner warmth from the contact.

As the others moved away, Sarah stayed back. 'I will get you some food later and you can sleep again in the barn,' she said to the boy. 'And I will try to get you a warm sweater and some socks.' She hesitated a moment, then added: 'They were all delighted to meet you. Thank you for sharing your lovely thoughts with us.' The boy smiled his thanks.

'Well, I will see you later,' she added. And then, with a touch of embarrassment, she said quietly: 'God bless.'

She hurried after the others and caught up with Gillian and Betty walking silently along. She was keen to know what they had thought of Rowan.

'He's lovely,' replied Gillian, enthralled. 'Just lovely.'

'Pity he's only twelve,' remarked Betty, who was fourteen. 'He would make a lovely boy-friend.'

'Is that all you can think of?' snapped Gillian.

'No. I just meant he's special, very special. He must have been very well educated – he knows such a lot about things. What do you feel about him, Sarah?'

'Well, he has a certain quality,' Sarah replied airily, not wishing to let them know how much she loved him. 'I couldn't say he's cool, though.'

They laughed at this, for 'cool', 'dead-on' or 'deadly' were usually the words they used for something special. Now they all felt these words sounded shallow and empty when you wanted to express real admiration for something.

'I'm going into the village to the second-hand clothes shop to get him some clothes,' said Sarah. 'Have you any money on you, Gillian? I've only a pound.'

'I can give you two pounds. I got four for baby-sitting last night.'

'I can let you have seventy pence,' added Betty.

'Listen, Betty and I will get them and bring them to you tomorrow,' suggested Gillian.

'That would be great. The evenings are getting colder and the poor fellow doesn't have a stitch of his own.'

'How come?' asked Betty.

'I don't really know. He must have just run away leaving everything behind,' Sarah said casually.

'What will we buy?' asked Gillian.

'A sweater. It must be big and make sure it's wool. A jacket if you have enough money. And socks ... oh, and don't buy anything black.'

'Why not?' asked Betty. 'It's very fashionable.'

'I don't exactly know why,' answered Sarah, 'but I feel he wouldn't want black. I can't explain – just trust me.'

'Okay. I don't know which of you is the strange one, you or him,' Betty said. They smiled at each other and parted.

Sarah hurried home and joined the others at tea. Gran had made lots of scones and a boiled cake and there was plenty of home-made jam. They all sat around quietly. Mr Robinson was reading the evening paper.

'Would you please pass the brown bread, Mary?'

'Here you are, Sarah. Would you like another scone, Jamie?'

'Oh, yes, please. Thank you, Sarah.'

Mr Robinson, listening to all this unaccustomed politeness, looked over his glasses. 'What's happening around here?' he asked. 'No screaming at one another? What did you put in those scones, Gran?'

Gran looked up with a blank expression on her face and the children burst into loud laughter.

Chapter 5

Sarah had just finished the washing-up after tea. She cut two slices of Gran's cake and took a banana from the fruit bowl, then filled a plastic container with orange juice.

Her father had gone down to the Angler's Rest pub for the evening. Sticking her head round the door, she could see Gran sitting in her favourite chair, with Jamie perched on the arm. Mary and Bingo were lying on the floor and there was an interesting film on the television to keep them occupied.

Putting on a warm sweater and her overcoat, and pulling on her wellies, she slipped quietly out the kitchen door.

The evening was still but there was a chill in the air. The sky was studded with twinkling stars and there was a pale ring round the moon. Sarah could see her breath as she blew on her hands. 'It will be cold tonight,' she said to herself, as she crossed the shadowy farmyard.

As she was about to open the gate, she heard the sound of a bike on the gravel and saw a faint yellow light. Oh, no, she thought, that will be Brendan O'Keeffe. She was just about to duck down behind the pillars when the bike scrunched to a halt. Brendan dismounted.

He was in Sarah's class in school. He had few friends and he was usually teased and bullied by the other boys about his awful haircuts and his ears that stuck out. Worst of all, he had a bad stammer which was more noticeable when he became excited or embarrassed.

Some of the boys called him 'Dumbo' or even 'Duh ... Duh ... Dumbo!' Sarah felt sorry for him and sometimes took his side when the others were jeering at him. The result was that Brendan took a shine to her. He would wait after school for her and he would cycle over to see her once or twice a week.

Sarah wasn't too pleased and sometimes she would stay back after school to avoid him, but she couldn't bring herself to be rude to his face.

One day his parents stopped her in the village to thank her for her kindness to him. They explained that he had been very ill when he was an infant. She remembered this when her friends shrugged him off and advised her to tell him to get lost.

'G ... G ... Good evening, Sarah,' he said, as he took off his bicycle clips. 'It's like winter, isn't it?'

'Yes, you shouldn't be out on a night like this. You

might catch cold.'

'Oh, Oh, I'm fine, thank you, S ... S ... Sarah. I enjoyed the ride up.' He looked at Sarah and then at the bike.

'D ... D ... Did you notice anything new about my bike?' he asked.

'Oh, yes,' she exclaimed, pretending to be excited, because she knew how devoted Brendan was to his mountain bike. Bending down, she ran her finger along the new luminous stickers on the crossbar.

'They're fab. Where did you get them?'

Pleased with her response, Brendan explained how they had arrived that very day in the bicycle shop and that he had been the first to buy them.

'Well, they're very nice, Brendan, but I have to go now. I have to meet someone.'

Brendan's face fell. He produced a large bar of chocolate and handed it to her.

'Oh, you're too kind, Brendan. You shouldn't keep buying chocolate for me as I'll only get spots. But thank you.'

He tried to say something but his stammer defeated him. She encouraged him: 'Take your time, Brendan. Now what were you going to say?'

After a few more attempts, he explained that he had come to ask her to the cinema the following day. 'Your favourite star is in it. I know you'd l ... l ... love it.'

'I'm afraid I'm busy tomorrow, perhaps next week. I really must go now. Thanks for coming.'

'B ... But I just travelled three m ... m ... miles to see you.'

Sarah was feeling guilty at this stage.

'Brendan, I'm going over to the woods to see someone, and he's waiting.'

Brendan frowned, feeling rejected.

'I didn't know you had a boyfriend.'

'No, it's nothing like that; he's only twelve; he just needs my help.' She felt there was not much point in denying Rowan's existence as some of the others would tell Brendan sooner or later.

As Sarah passed through the gate, Brendan insisted on walking with her.

'Just to the wood,' Sarah said firmly.

'I'll bring my lamp so we can see,' Brendan suggested.

Sarah accepted. She knew that if her Gran was looking for her she would see Brendan's bike and assume they were together.

As they walked over the silver fields their feet made crunching sounds in the frosty grass. Near the lodge, Joe, the farmhand, lit up a cigarette and watched their progress. As they reached the edge of the woods, Sarah stopped.

'Thanks, Brendan, for walking me this far. You'd better head home now; it's getting late.'

Brendan looked across to the dark and silent wood. Nervously, he asked was she really going in there.

Sarah's eyes wandered around the darkness of the

wood. 'Oh, yes, I just love this place, day or night.'

'I would be very c … c … cautious if I were you,' he said, peering fearfully at the wood. Then Brendan suddenly looked physically shook as if he had just seen a ghost. 'B … B … B … Behind y … y … you.'

Sarah turned quickly. The boy was standing behind her.

'Sorry if I frightened you. I was just walking up from the beach.'

'Well, you did give us a start. This is my friend Brendan.'

'Delighted to meet you,' said the boy, extending his hand in friendship. Brendan nervously took the hand, which appeared cold, yet transmitted a warm surge through Brendan's body.

'This is Rowan.'

Brendan cleared his throat. 'I … I'm de … de … delighted to m … make your acquaintance. W … Well, I'll be off,' Brendan flustered. 'I don't want to b … be late home.'

'Goodbye, Brendan, see you tomorrow,' Sarah said amiably.

'Goodbye, Brendan,' said the boy, placing a hand on his shoulder. Brendan felt a little embarrassed.

Then the boy's hand gently moved to his throat. Brendan felt dizzy and closed his eyes. It was just like drinking some beautiful liquid, he thought. He could almost sense it coursing down his throat; it was wonderful and soothing.

The boy slowly removed his hand. With a mixture of

confusion and amazement, Brendan turned and hurried away.

They looked after him.

'Poor Brendan! I really feel sorry for him. He's got a good heart but he always seems to have problems. Even his Dad gives him a tough time about his stammer. "He doesn't get it from our side of the family", he tells his wife.

'Brendan told me that in confidence,' she went on. 'I guess I'm the only one he tells about his home life. Oh, I am going on a bit ...' she smiled thinly. 'I'm sure you don't want to know all the problems of everyone in the village.'

The boy was silent.

Sarah wondered why he'd touched Brendan's throat.

'I have something to show you,' he said softly. They hurried to the middle of the wood and sat in silence beside their favourite oak tree. Sarah was very curious to know what they were waiting for. 'You'll see in a minute,' he insisted.

They waited quietly in the dark silence. Then movement could be heard in the undergrowth and a badger suddenly emerged in the half-light, its grey coat harmonising with the grey tones of the wood.

Sarah had to stifle a shout of excitement, for she had never seen a badger, except a dead one on the road.

It sniffed the air and circled cautiously, then moved towards them. Sarah's heart was pounding with excitement and tension. Closer and closer it came until it began to sniff at her foot. Then it placed its head on the boy's lap.

Sarah gazed in disbelief. Badgers were normally such shy and retiring creatures. As she was getting used to it, a second came out to join the first. The boy was holding their heads and brushing down their hair. They were busy trying to climb up on him like playful puppies.

'They are charming creatures, aren't they?' he said.

'Oh, yes, absolutely.'

Suddenly Sarah saw another animal approaching. Prowling stealthily like a cat, it moved, almost concealed by the darkness. It stopped and stared, amber eyes watching the boy and girl at play with the badgers. Then it cautiously moved to the clearing. Sarah blurted out. 'Wow! a fox …'

It froze momentarily, then trotted across to the boy. It, too, began to be playful and rolled about. Sarah nervously brushed the golden-red fur. She was intrigued. What a pleasure to be so close to these beautiful creatures of the wood.

Before the evening was over, a hare had also joined them and, as if to cap it all, a long-eared owl flew through the gloom on hushed wings, swooped down and landed on the boy's shoulder. Ruffling its mottled buff plumage, it blinked orange eyes and settled itself.

'This is the most exciting day of my life,' Sarah exclaimed.

'I'm glad,' the boy responded. 'You showed me their

homes and now I'm glad to be able to show you the creatures themselves.'

'Nobody would believe this if I told them,' she laughed. 'They would say I made it all up. It's truly fantastic. I would love Mr Hughes, the librarian, to try to photograph this ... he'd probably pass out with excitement.'

They sat for a long time, the warmth from the animals' bodies making them cosy, despite the chill of the night winds.

'Oh, I completely forgot,' Sarah frowned in annoyance. 'Your food!'

She produced the cake and the orange juice from the plastic bag and they shared the food, throwing pieces to the fox and the badgers.

'You know ...' Sarah shook her head sorrowfully, 'animals get very badly treated at times by humans. I can't understand it. People shoot them, poison them, trap them, even do experiments on them ... it's awful!' She flared up with a mixture of anger and grief, and a tear ran down her cheek. She tried to cover it up with a smile.

'That's the second time you've seen me crying. I'm sorry.' Her frown deepened. 'It's just that when I look at these lovely creatures sitting around with us, I can't help being reminded of the cruelty of humans.'

'You are a very sensitive person, Sarah. That's a rare quality. Don't ever be embarrassed by it.'

Then, reflecting on what Sarah had said, he spoke

firmly: 'Man has reasoning and choice, which are impossible for animals. Violence only coarsens human feeling and destroys tenderness, and this leads to the brutalising of the human species.'

His voice dropped. 'We all share the responsibility for the degrading effects of cruelty.' Sarah observed his face, which looked so sad.

'But it's difficult to convince people that tenderness is not weakness ...'

His expression changed, as if seeing some great horror. 'Mankind is piling upon itself a huge debt by its continuing cruelty to the animal kingdom.'

Sarah did not fully understand what he meant, so she probed a little further. 'Is it okay for scientists to experiment?'

'No individuals or groups must allow themselves to be licensed torturers of the rest of creation,' he said firmly.

Then, he brightened up and breathed softly. 'Compassion can awaken in the heart the vision of the oneness of life.'

Sarah sat silent, enthralled by his words.

'Your lovely thoughts should be shared with everyone,' she whispered. 'You are so good.'

He looked embarrassed.

'No, I mean it, you are really good, she went on. 'I don't mean goody-goody but really good, the way all human beings should be.'

He responded with a smile. 'Remember that "human"

means "enlightened one".'

'It's getting late, we'd better go,' Sarah said suddenly.

The animals departed after several hugs and strokes along their fur, and the last to leave was the owl. They watched him winging his way across the fields, then they hurried back to the barn.

Sarah gave the boy a kiss on the cheek and went to the house.

As she lay in bed thinking about the lovely evening she had just experienced, she heard her father arriving in from the pub. He sat down in the kitchen. She knew he had taken a lot of drink by the amount of noise he made disturbing chairs and cupboards.

Then things became quiet for a time until she heard him calling to his wife in the empty night and sobbing loudly.

Sarah wanted to rush down the stairs and hug him but they didn't do that sort of thing any more. She just lay quietly listening to his sighs. Tears ran down her face onto the pillow.

Chapter 6

Sarah sat with her family near the front of the church. It was the early Mass and many of the local families were present. Gran sat beside Jamie, her arthritic fingers clutching her red rosary beads.

Mr Robinson shifted uncomfortably in his seat. God and Mass meant very little to him any more since the death of his wife. Only for his mother's nagging and persuading he would never come.

Still, he enjoyed meeting a few of his old friends outside the church. St Michael's boasted a beautiful stained-glass window of the Archangel and, when the sun shone through it, shafts of rainbow light danced on the pews.

Sarah smiled as she watched Con Hughes, the librarian, do the first reading.

'A reading from the letter of Saint Paul to the Colossians.

For in Him all things were created,
In heaven and on earth,
Visible and invisible.
Whether Thrones or Dominions or
Principalities or Authorities.
All things were created through Him
And for Him. He is before all things,
And in Him all things hold together.

There was something about this reading that seemed to strike a chord in Sarah. She stared at the large window and the face of the Archangel looked somehow familiar; it looked like the boy's face, only older. She nudged Mary, indicating for her to look up.

Mary looked at the window and smiled at Sarah. Sarah nudged her again, trying to get her to look really hard. Gran threw a disapproving glance at Sarah.

When Mass was over, Sarah decided to wait and ask the curate some questions. Fr Keating was very popular in the community, always involved in charities and sporting events. It was hard to tell he was a priest for he never wore his clerical clothes, except on Sundays, at weddings or funerals.

Sarah knew that after Mass he would be going for coffee in the community hall. He was a very handsome athletic type who was always telling jokes and funny stories. Sarah waited until he sat down, and lingered for several more moments until he was on his own. He kept throwing asides about the football match to one of the local team captains, bringing peals of laughter. Sarah moved nervously towards him.

'Fr Keating,' she said quietly.

'Oh, hello, Sarah. How are you?'

'Fine, thanks. Would you mind if I joined you for a moment?'

'Of course, except I must watch the time. I will be helping at the next Mass and celebrating the twelve-thirty.'

'Oh, it won't take a moment,' insisted Sarah.

'Well, what is it, young lady? I don't normally have the pleasure of your company, or indeed of any of the teenagers in the village at this hour of the morning. Now, if it was a disco in the local hall we'd get them there in their droves, but ask them to make the early Mass and they'll find some excuse,' he said flatly. 'Oh, they will be at evening Mass okay, standing at the back and leaving half-way through the service.'

Sarah really wanted to ask him a few questions, not talk about the problems of the parish.

'Well, I suppose you'd better tell me what's bothering you, young lady. If it's something very serious, perhaps you could call in to the presbytery at two-thirty?'

'No, it's not serious, it's just ... Fr Keating, could you please tell me something about angels!?'

He broke into a broad grin and looked at her doubtfully.

'Well now, Sarah, I would have thought that angels

would be the furthest thing from the minds of you young people nowadays. U2, or David Bowie, would be more like it. So would you kindly tell your friends that two windows were broken in the church hall after the last disco, and cider bottles were strewn all over the green. Now this is very serious. Fr Sheppard was very annoyed and the local sergeant will be visiting a few homes in the next few days. So keep out of trouble like a good girl. I must be off.' He swallowed a last mouthful of coffee. 'Bye, Sarah. Nice talking with you.'

Sarah tried to pursue her question but the priest hurried away.

'Hmm …' she said to herself, 'he didn't even want to discuss it.'

Gillian and Betty were outside, sitting on the wall. 'Hi!' they greeted each other.

'I got the clothes and a pair of hiking boots that should fit Rowan.'

'That's great,' said Sarah.

Betty laughed.

'It's amazing! Here we are, buying clothes, sheltering and feeding a perfect stranger. If anyone said a month ago I'd be doing this, I'd have told them they were nuts!'

'Yes, I know what you mean,' said Sarah.

'*Perfect* stranger is right,' added Gillian, reflecting on the boy.

'Do you believe in angels?' Sarah asked, confidentially.

Betty replied doubtfully. 'I know he is a lovely, kind

person, but an angel! Now, that's going a bit far.'

Gillian piped up: 'Maybe he's an alien from outer space. After all, you did see some bright light in the wood the night he arrived.'

'Don't be silly,' said Sarah. 'He's not an alien.'

'It's no sillier than saying he is an angel,' retorted Betty.

'Yes. I guess you're right, but I think we should try and find out, don't you?'

They both nodded in agreement. 'I tried to ask Fr Keating this morning but I didn't get too far.'

'Perhaps you should speak to the parish priest. My mother told me he's lived all over the world. If anyone should know it would be him.'

'Good idea, Betty. We will talk to him, and to your vicar, Gillian, and tomorrow we will check out some information in the library.'

'This is exciting,' said Gillian.

*   *   *

Sarah brought the clothes back to the barn but Rowan wasn't there, so she left them hidden in the hay. After lunch she and the other girls called to the parish priest's house.

Fr Sheppard was a quiet man in his late sixties, with silver hair and a friendly face. But he tended to keep to himself and some people considered him a bit stand-offish.

The housekeeper opened the door and looked suspiciously at the girls. Sarah nervously asked if Father Sheppard was in. Mrs Riordan's eyes scanned the girls' faces, then said, 'Fr Sheppard usually takes a short rest after his lunch …'

She could see how keen the girls were to speak to him. 'Well,' she continued, 'I'll just check whether he can see you or not.'

Fr Sheppard agreed to see them. They were brought into a large room, full of books. Some holy pictures hung on the walls, and a warm coal fire was burning brightly.

They sat near Fr Sheppard, who ordered home-made lemonade and biscuits for them, while he sipped his favourite port. They sat silently on the edge of the large sofa, gulping down the lemonade.

'Enjoying that?' asked Fr Sheppard, breaking the silence.

Sarah was about to speak when the clock chimed three. 'You have a question you want answered, am I right?'

'Oh, yes,' they said in chorus. 'Do you know anything about angels? Well, what we mean is … do they exist, for example, and, if they do, how would we recognise one …?'

Fr Sheppard said nothing but looked over his half-glasses.

'Angels!' he said quietly, as if they had touched on a subject close to his heart.

'Yes,' said Gillian, 'we're doing a kind of project.'

'Yes … a survey,' added Betty.

'How very interesting,' said Fr Sheppard. 'Well, you know our church is named after Lord Michael, that great

Archangel whom we call on to protect us from the evil one.'

He could see that they were genuine in their enquiries, so he continued: 'Human beings are not God's only creation. Between the perfect God and the unfinished imperfect man are God's shining emissaries whom we call angels. "Angel" is the Greek word for "messenger of God".

'Angels are of a higher development than man,' he went on. 'Throughout recorded history very many races and religions have accepted angelic visitations – the Egyptians, Romans, Greeks, Persians, Muslims, Hindus, Jewish Kabbalists, Japanese Shintoists, and many of the primitive peoples of the world. Of course, both the Old and the New Testaments give tribute to the selfless service of angels.'

Sarah and her friends looked pleased, even though they hadn't really understood half of what he had said.

'I hope this is clear, what I'm saying ...'

'Oh, yes,' they replied. 'It's fascinating, please go on.'

'Well, it's refreshing to find young people so enthusiastic about the subject.' Then he continued. 'The great seers have shown us there are nine heavenly hierarchies – the Cherubim, the Seraphim, the Thrones, the Principalities, the Powers and Mights, the Archai, the Archangels and the Angels. All are working to serve God and help man by guiding him along the path of spiritual understanding. To put it simply, we do believe in angels. They are not to be worshipped, only loved, as you would love a special friend who is always there to assist you. In the words of the Psalm 91.11: "He hath given his angels charge over thee to keep thee in all thy ways".'

They left, thanking him for all his interesting information. Fr Sheppard closed the door behind them; he had enjoyed the talk as much as the girls. It was sad, he thought, that adults led such complicated lives and lost the bright vision of their youth.

The girls had not gone far when, to their surprise and delight, they met the Reverend Jones, who was briskly walking his dog.

They hurried up alongside him.

'Good afternoon, Vicar,' said Gillian.

He tipped his hat. 'Good afternoon, young ladies.'

'May we walk along with you and ask you a few questions?'

'Of course,' came the Reverend Jones's reply.

'Well, we are doing a project on angels and we were wondering if you could say something about them.'

Reverend Jones looked a bit taken aback by their frank question. 'Well, let me see,' he pondered.

'Angels were created before humans. They are holy messengers possessing exquisite beauty and deep truth; they live on a higher plane than we do. They have communicated with and helped the human race down through its long history. But they never interfere with free will. They respect human freedom. They only come by invitation, with willing co-operation from both sides.

'On the other hand, the powers of darkness have no compunction about taking possession of mind, body and soul. They can even appear as angels of light, and are more likely to be roaming the world. So let that be a warning to you young people who may delve too deeply into these things. One should never play around with ouija boards or the likes. One can get very badly burned, if you take my meaning.'

'Oh, yes, thank you. Well, we'll be off now; thanks again, Vicar.'

'Oh dear, that was a little worrying,' remarked Gillian, 'what he said about dark spirits appearing as angels of light. I hope he didn't think we were up to anything weird like ouija boards and things.'

'Well, I suppose he doesn't get people coming up to him every day talking about angels,' said Betty. 'I don't believe Rowan's anything but good and, if it turned out that he really was an angel, I know he would be an angel of light. Let's go to him,' and they hurried down the road.

*   *   *

Vaso finished the last drop from the plastic cider bottle, scrunched it up and kicked it over a wall into a garden.

'You finished it all,' said Kicker, annoyed.

'Well, so what?' said Vaso. 'Wanna make something of it?'

'No, Vaso.'

'Good! Right!' said Vaso menacingly.

Hammer pointed down the road. 'Look who's coming.'

The three of them stepped off the path and onto the road. Brendan braked to a halt.

'Oh, hello, Vincent. I mean Vaso.' The three of them were in the same class as Brendan in school.

'Well, if it isn't Duh ... Duh ... Dumbo! You should be flying, not on a bike.' Hammer lifted the back of the bike up by the carrier. Brendan winced with pain and carefully dismounted. 'Please leave me alone.'

'Please leave me alone,' mimicked Kicker.

Then Vaso grabbed Brendan by the lapels and pulled his scout's tie out from his sweater.

'How come you're not stuttering as per usual, hey?' he said, pulling and twisting hard on the white shirt.

'Stop, you're hurting me,' pleaded Brendan.

'Have you any money on you, D ... Dumbo?' said Hammer.

'No,' replied Brendan, red in the face.

'Well, we don't believe you.'

They pulled him to the ground, then Hammer, being the strongest, pulled up his legs, making a couple of coins roll from his pocket along the pavement.

Hammer shook him again. This time a large bar of chocolate fell from Brendan's coat pocket. Kicker grabbed the bar, pulled the wrapper off it and took a bite.

Vaso yanked it from Kicker and took an even bigger bite.

'Leave a bit for me,' shouted Hammer, and Vaso threw him a piece.

Brendan began to whimper. 'That was for my friend.'

'We know all about your friend. Now I asked you, how come you don't have your stammer?'

'It's a secret,' said Brendan. This made the others laugh.

'Well, tell us,' said Vaso. 'What's the big secret? Your stammer wasn't a secret; the whole village knew about it. How come it's gone? It was there yesterday; D … did you lose it?' he said in a mocking tone.

'What?' said Brendan.

'You heard me,' yelled Vaso, 'I don't stutter.'

Then Vaso pushed Brendan's arm up behind his back, causing him to scream with pain.

'It was Sarah Robinson's friend.'

'Who?'

'Sarah Robinson's friend. He's a mysterious stranger who cured my stammer.'

Vaso threw a glance of disbelief at his friends. 'How did he do this amazing feat? By magic or what?' he pushed Brendan's arm higher.

'By touching my neck. Honest,' said Brendan.

Seeing the commotion, a man came out of his house and yelled at the three lads.

'Leave him alone, you young pups, or I'll take a strap to you. Do you hear me?'

Brendan staggered to his feet, adjusting his tie and glasses.

'I'll be telling your fathers about this,' said the man.

'Big deal,' said Vaso under his breath.

'Now clear off.'

'Keep the head, Pops,' said Kicker as they strolled away.

Brendan thanked the man and hurried away on his bicycle.

* * *

Sarah and her friends ducked down along the farm wall for fear that Gran, who could be seen through the kitchen window, would call her. They hurried along till they reached the gate and walked up the fields.

As they got near the wood, Vaso, Kicker and Hammer appeared, along with lots of the children from the village.

Sarah, Gillian and Betty tried to ignore them and walk past. Then Vaso stepped out in front of them. Taking his hands from his pockets, he pulled the cigarette from his lips and flicked it away.

Sarah, not wanting to make eye contact, stared at his sweater. It had the word 'Metallica' written across it.

Realising what she was doing he zipped up his biker jacket and flicked his long black curly hair. They seemed to be standing for ages, then, looking hard at her he asked: 'Where is he?'

Sarah tried to pass off the question by saying she didn't know what he meant.

'I asked you, where is he?' repeated Vaso, annoyed now.

Tossing her head, and feigning innocence Sarah asked: 'Who do you mean?'

'E.T! Who do you think I mean?!'

This brought a nervous laugh from the rest. 'Now listen, Scarface, I'm going to ask you one more time. Where is this "space cadet"?'

'I told you, Vaso Healy, I don't know who you mean.'

Vaso slapped Sarah hard across the face.

'Leave my sister alone,' yelled Jamie, and he ran over and began to kick Vaso in the leg. Vaso pushed him on the ground.

'Leave him alone,' said a voice behind Vaso. Vaso quickly turned to find out who dared challenge him.

The boy stood still, his golden curls blowing in the chilly wind. Vaso, flanked by Hammer and Kicker, stepped up to him. 'So, you're the big mystery around here! Show him how you got your name, Hammer.'

Hammer was about to butt the boy with his head but suddenly stopped after looking into his eyes.

'What's the matter?' said Vaso, annoyed. 'Are you afraid of this little weed?'

He looked at Kicker, who also stepped back. So Vaso, feeling really annoyed, swung out with his hand and hit the boy hard on the face. The boy didn't flinch.

Vaso swung again, harder this time; still the boy didn't move. Vaso stared into the boy's eyes, then noticed a trickle of blood running from the boy's nose, and across his lips. Vaso was about to strike again but something stopped him. He trembled inwardly.

Then the rest of the children shouted: 'Leave him alone.'

Vaso turned around and glared at them, and they all stared back. He turned again to the boy, whose blue eyes seemed to pierce Vaso's brain. He stepped back and shouted to Hammer and Kicker. 'Let's get out of here.'

They ran as fast as they could down the field. Then, from behind the hedge came Brendan. They all walked slowly to the wood.

Joe, the farmhand, had been watching the whole thing through binoculars from a distance. 'There's something fishy going on here; perhaps I ought to have a word with Bill,' he mumbled to himself.

*   *   *

They moved into the centre of the wood and sat around the boy. So many children and young people made Sarah nervous. She wanted the boy to herself yet she knew she mustn't be selfish.

There was an awkward silence because of the incident. But the boy didn't seem to be put out by what had happened.

One of the older boys spoke up.

'He's not really a bad fellow; Vaso, I mean. He tries to be tough; he can be mean at times, but he can be kind too. The way he looks after his racing pigeons, he's very caring towards them.'

'It's good to hear that,' said the boy.

Then a girl asked: 'Where are you from?'

'Far away, yet as close as one room is to another,'

answered the boy.

'Why didn't you hit back at Vaso?' asked another.

'All violence is dragging down the human race. We must not add to violence, only heal the scars it causes.'

'But there's violence everywhere, especially on television and films,' remarked someone.

'The constant stressing of violence and cruelty in the media, or anywhere else, bores deep into our psyche. We must use our hearts to balance our actions and develop a hurt-free attitude.'

'But what about writers, photographers, painters, even musicians? They can show us violence as well. What do you say about that?'

'We must accept that we are fully responsible for all we write, speak, create or do, whether poet or soldier.'

'Can you prove all this to be true?' the lad who had spoken up for Vaso asked.

'There is no argument that can prove or disprove the truth. Cruelty and violence can be of so many varieties. For example, making war weapons causes poverty somewhere, even if these weapons are never used. We can damage things, not only by physical pollution but also by mental pollution, because the thought comes first, then the action.'

All the children were very attentive to the boy and explained to him how they had seen programmes on television about the different things that were happening to the planet.

One girl put up her hand, as if in school, and said very quietly. 'Some things happen by accident.'

There was a pause, then she continued. 'My father's farm has a lovely lake. We used to see lots of swans on it. People would fish there as well. But a new factory, built nearby, accidentally spilled chemicals into it. All the fish were killed and now it's too dangerous even to swim there anymore. My dad was very upset but he couldn't prove that it was the company that had polluted it.

'He had to put signs warning that the lake was dangerous.' Then she added: 'But he still loves to walk there in the evening.'

The boy seemed sad as he listened to the young girl tell her story.

'Is there anything that can be done?' asked Sarah.

The boy did not respond at once but then said with a smile: 'Let's try a little God-science.'

'What's that?' asked Jamie, who was nearest to the boy.

'Follow me.'

They all stood up. He asked the girl to lead the way to the lake. They walked through the wood, then over several fields. The evening was creeping in, so the boy put on the sweater he had been given by the girls.

Finally they reached the lake. A grey mist shrouded the water and glided like a shadowy ghoul across its surface. There was an eerie silence as the feeble light retreated over the hills. The darkness of night approaching the barren fields seemed to match the dreary atmosphere.

'It looks very spooky,' said one of the children.

The boy asked the children to form a circle around the lake, which they did. Some of them felt a little strange about the idea of holding hands, but they did it when he asked. Rooks and jackdaws flew over, calling loudly, but the boy held his concentration.

Then they all felt a strange tingling in their arms. It was a beautiful sensation, but it made their bodies tremble as if a current of energy was passing through them. A circle of blue-white light appeared above their heads, radiating outwards in constant motion.

The children seemed strengthened by the bond of touch as the light continued to encircle them. They were dazzled by its beauty.

Throbbing and flowing, it appeared to enlarge and renew its circle, the healing rays stretching out over the whole lake. The super-physical currents intensified until the children had to close their eyes.

Then the circle of light descended lower and lower until it sank below the water. Different-coloured rays emanated from the lake. Flashes of purple, blue, yellow and green shot horizontally and vertically through the dark waters, penetrating deeper and deeper until every molecule was touched by the healing light.

Then the water became crystal blue. A fragrant breeze touched the children's nostrils, and they gently let go of each other's hands.

The boy looked physically shaken. The children broke

the circle and hurried back to where he was.

'That was the most amazing thing I ever saw,' said the young girl whose father owned the lake.

'It's time we all went home,' said Sarah.

As they walked silently across the darkened field, they heard the noisy wingbeat of mute swans. They looked up and watched four swans fly overhead, and land in the quiet waters. The place took on an enchanted mood as the creatures casually floated about. No more was said as they headed home.

*　　　*　　　*

Vaso had vented his anger on Mrs Wyer, who had reported him for drinking cider, by throwing a large brick through her bedroom window.

Running down the laneway with Hammer and Kicker, they had turned the corner only to be met by Vaso's younger brother, Jimmy. As they caught their breath Jimmy said quietly, 'I have some bad news, Vaso.'

'What?' yelled Vaso, sensing it was something to do with his birds.

'The cat from next door got into the loft and has killed most of the birds.'

'Oh, no!' sobbed Vaso. 'Is Swifty all right?' Swifty was his favourite pigeon which had won several races and earned over fifty pounds.

'He's not dead,' said Jimmy. 'But he's badly damaged. I don't think he's going to make it. Dad phoned the vet but he's away until Tuesday.'

Vaso paced up and down, trying to conceal his tears. Brendan cycled past and sensed something was wrong.

'What's the matter?' he asked, as if the incident between them earlier had never happened.

Jimmy told him the story.

'Oh, that's terrible,' said Brendan, showing genuine sympathy.

Vaso and the others ignored Brendan who climbed back on his bike and was about to move off, but stopped, looked at Vaso and said quite casually: 'Why don't you bring the bird to Sarah Robinson's friend? I'm sure he can help.'

'Get lost, Dumbo!' yelled Vaso.

Chapter 7

A light rain began to fall. Sarah glanced at the kitchen window, watching the drops gently tap on the glass and run down the pane. She had just made two cheese sandwiches and placed them carefully in a plastic container. Looking around the door, she could see Gran asleep in the armchair. Mary and Jamie were in bed and her dad had gone down to the local for a quiet pint.

Taking a carton of milk from the fridge she was about to pour some out when she heard a loud knocking on the kitchen door. It made her jump and spill milk across the oiled tablecloth.

Who could that be? she wondered.

Another loud knock.

She tried to peer out the window to see who was outside, when a face suddenly looked in at her, making her recoil in fright.

Sarah carefully lifted the latch and peeped around the

door. Vaso stood outside in the rain, holding a shoebox in his hand.

'Oh … Vincent,' said Sarah. 'What do you want?'

Vaso stood there trembling, his long hair matted across his face by the rain.

'Can I see … your friend?' he asked with a tremor in his voice. 'It's important. Please!'

'Stand in out of the rain,' said Sarah looking in at Gran who was still dozing in front of the television.

'I'm just about to go to him,' she remarked, then throwing her coat over her head she led Vaso to the barn.

The boy sat high in the loft holding a barn-owl in his hand.

Sarah and Vaso looked in amazement.

'I didn't know we had barn-owls roosting here,' said Sarah. The boy smiled and made a slight movement with his hand. The owl lifted off and flew up into the rafters.

'I brought you some food.'

'Thank you,' said the boy.

Vaso said nothing but stood and stared. Then Sarah said awkwardly: 'You remember Vincent?'

The boy climbed down from the bales of hay and extended his hand in friendship. Vaso wiped the hair from his eyes, then rubbed his hands along his jeans. Slowly he offered his hand. There was an immediate feeling of friendship in the handshake.

'Was there something you wanted to show me?' asked the boy.

Vaso's eyes stared at him, then he carefully pulled the lid off the shoebox to reveal a pigeon whose wing was nearly torn off and had some feathers missing from its breast. Vaso gritted his teeth as his eyes misted over.

'Oh dear,' said Sarah. 'The poor thing.'

'Jesus Christ, that bleedin' cat,' yelled Vaso.

The boy took the bird gently from the box and looked deep into Vaso's eyes.

'Never use a sacred name except in prayer.'

Vaso and Sarah were taken aback by this comment.

'There is a power in sacred words that must not be abused. You may need that power some day.'

Vaso watched the boy gently stroke the lifeless bird.

The boy then closed his eyes and breathed on it. Suddenly the bird stirred and began to rouse itself. It flapped its wings and flew onto Vaso's head.

Vaso could not believe his eyes. He lifted the bird from his head and carefully examined it. There was no sign of a tear or wound.

'How can I ever thank you?'

The boy pondered for a moment then said: 'I want you to repair the broken window and do something extra, in return, for the lady.'

Sarah looked blankly, but Vaso knew exactly what he meant.

'It'll be awkward,' said Vaso, 'but I'll do my best.'

Then he returned the bird to the box, thanked the boy and headed home.

Chapter 8

After school, Sarah, Gillian and Betty headed for the local library. Con Hughes, the librarian, was going out the door with a camera.

'Good afternoon, Con,' said Sarah. He greeted them with a certain reserve.

'Off to take some snaps?' asked Gillian.

'Well, yes, as a matter of fact. I'm going to investigate a strange light that was seen near Tierney's lake yesterday.' The girls smiled broadly.

'Oh, you may laugh,' he remarked. 'I hope it doesn't end up like that "wildcat" episode. I haven't forgotten that, Sarah Robinson.'

Sarah asked if the library had any books on angels.

Con Hughes looked at her suspiciously. 'There are lots of books on fairy tales and folklore on the far wall of the library.'

'No, we mean about real angels.'

'Well, there probably is something in the religious section. Or you could try the Old Masters. They depicted a lot of angels in their paintings. Oh, come with me,' he said with a sigh.

'There,' he said, pulling out various books on the Old Masters. 'Botticelli, Leonardo da Vinci, Raphael, Fra Angelico, Giotto, Rembrandt and more recent works, William Blake, Edward Burne-Jones, Block. Plenty of angels to find in there.'

'Thanks.'

'Angels, indeed,' said Con. 'Now be sure to put those books back in their places, you hear?'

'Yes, of course we will,' said Betty.

They looked at all the amazing paintings, most of which they had never seen before. As they pored over the images they began to see, emerging from these masterpieces, a resemblance to the boy.

It wasn't so much in the appearance as in the feeling. They couldn't explain it, but they felt instinctively that there was a connection with Rowan's beauty and what the artists had tried to capture, whether in an icon or in a Pre-Raphaelite painting.

Yet they couldn't prove anything; they simply had to trust their intuition. There was no doubt that the boy was gifted and possessed healing powers. They had read about people who claimed to have 'the cure'. They had witnessed his powers, yet to believe he was an angel was as outrageous as to believe he was an extra-terrestrial.

Whatever the answer, they were all happy he was here.

As they walked down the road the girls could not believe their eyes, for there was Vaso with his dad, watched by Kicker and Hammer, repairing a window in Mrs Wyer's home.

Mrs Wyer stood there, smiling, and had a tray full of tea and cakes for them. Vaso climbed down the ladder and walked over to Sarah.

'Hi,' he said quietly.

Gillian and Betty tried to ignore him, assuming Sarah would do the same.

'We're fixing the window I broke. Will you mention it to Rowan and tell him I sold some records to pay for the glass?'

Sarah smiled. 'How is the bird?'

'Oh, fine. Mr Davison is going to give me some fledglings next spring to replace the ones I lost.'

'Well, I'm glad all has worked out well for you.'

'I'd better go. Sorry for being such a pain. My dad and I are getting on real well all of a sudden, and it's all because of this window we're fixing. Crazy, isn't it? We're going to do some wall-papering and painting in Mrs Wyer's kitchen. So you can tell Rowan that as well. That's the "extra" thing he asked me to do.'

Mrs Wyer called Vincent over for his tea.

'He sure is a changed fellow in twenty-four hours,' remarked Betty.

'I think we all are,' replied Gillian.

* * *

Con Hughes was walking down from the lake. Sarah called to him. 'Did you see anything?'

He threw a glance at them in his usual suspicious way. 'No, I didn't. Yet it's curious. That lake is supposed to be badly polluted, but it is full of trout and there were swans, a grey heron and a pair of little grebes to be seen there. I got some good pictures. It will certainly make an interesting article in the local paper.'

Then he added, 'Well, did you put the books back?'

'Yes, thanks,' said Sarah.

'Why are the angels' faces all so similar in appearance?' asked Gillian.

'Well, that's called the classical style.'

'Could it be that some of the artists really saw angels?'

'Oh, I don't think so. It would have been just their imagination and their genius that produced these great works of art.'

Then he described how some of the artists had prayed, meditated and fasted before tackling some of their great works.

'Well, it's impossible to answer really. I'm afraid angels and the like have all been relegated to the realms of myth and fantasy, alongside fairies and goblins.'

Then, with a wry smile, he added: 'If you do see one, tell me. I would be delighted to photograph it,' and he walked away.

*   *   *

Sarah's father was checking his electric fence, as some of the sheep had wandered into his neighbour's field, when Joe came to join him.

'You know, Bill, I was talking to Frank Morris down at the sawmills. He said he would be interested in a bit of hardwood. I told him you had a couple of good specimens in the little wood, especially that large oak. He'd pay you handsomely for it. I'll take it down with the chainsaw if you like.'

'Well, I never really thought about touching the wood. Besides, the kids love exploring in there.'

'Sure there are plenty of other trees where they can run around. The money is as good in your pocket as wasting away over beyond where only a few squirrels benefit from it. You can't look a gift horse in the mouth, Bill.'

'Yes, perhaps you're right ... only that wood has been in the family for generations.'

'Can't become too sentimental about these things when there are always bills to pay. You might be able to buy a new barn instead of that old stone one.'

'Well, we'll see,' said Bill. 'Now help me with this ewe. She's gone and got herself stuck in the marsh.'

Later that afternoon Sarah was walking with the boy along the beach. She was telling him about Vincent repairing the window and how Con Hughes had gone to photograph the strange light over the lake. They both smiled at this.

'He's always hoping to become famous by taking a photograph of something rare or unusual. He even goes out with metal detectors, hoping he will find a rare object. He's mad to become famous, but he's really nice when you get to know him.'

The boy stared out to sea. His eyes swept the horizon as if looking for something, then he began to move to the water's edge.

Sarah watched with curiosity as the boy bent down and began to move his hands through the water in a rhythmic fashion.

'What are you doing?'

'I'm trying to call my friend,' he said. 'I'm sure you would like to meet him.'

'What is he?' asked Sarah, excitedly, having seen the way he was with the creatures of the wood.

'You'll just have to wait and see.' His hands, moving like antennae through the cold waters, had the power to attract and absorb energies from the ocean and channel them in whatever direction he chose. The forces of nature seemed to respond. Curlews flew close by, then small fish leaped from the water. The waves rippled and circled as he tuned in to the forces of nature.

He raised his hands from the water and the wind danced through his fingers. It was as if his hands were projecting love, greeting everything that approached.

As he emptied out his love in this form of communication, he immediately became filled with beneficial vibrations, capturing forces and relaying them to others, forces that cleanse, heal, restore, balance.

Sarah felt the energy and warmth seep into her.

*   *   *

The boy continued looking out to sea for a long time. Dimly at first, then gradually becoming sharply visible, a dorsal fin could be seen, cutting like a scythe through the surface of the waters, the body shearing undersea like some strange ethereal image. Then with a leap the dolphin cleared the white waves.

It could be seen clearly against the marble sea, shooting ahead of the waves. Followed by Sarah, the boy hurried out onto the rocks, the dolphin somersaulting in frenzied delight. They greeted each other with elegant, mysterious sounds. Then the boy stretched over and hugged the dolphin. Turning to Sarah he said: 'Say "hello" to my ocean sage.'

The dolphin greeted her with bouncing clicks.

Sarah stooped over and stroked the friendly creature.

'Did you know that his relation, the blue whale, is the largest creature ever to live on this planet?'

'That's amazing,' said Sarah. 'There is so much to discover, isn't there?'

'So much,' he reiterated. Then the dolphin, in less audible metallic clicks, whispered something to the boy. A tense expression crossed his face as he absorbed the information.

Turning to Sarah he said: 'I must go.'

'Oh no,' sighed Sarah.

The boy put his arms on her shoulders. 'Don't worry, I will be back. I have to do something that needs urgent attention.'

Sarah kissed him on the cheek. 'Be careful,' she whispered, then rubbed the dolphin affectionately. She felt very privileged to be in the boy's company. There was a confidence and sureness about life now.

The boy pulled off his sweater, shirt and shoes. 'Would you mind them for me, please?'

'Of course,' said Sarah.

He leaped into the water, then climbed onto the back of the dolphin.

'If only I had a camera,' sighed Sarah.

'Your mind is your camera,' replied the boy with a smile. Then they were off, knifing through the water, wave-riding, whirling and flickering, jumping clear of the water. On they moved, riders of the sea, the dolphin powerfully propelling them with exhilarating movements across the green, misty water. They were visible for about half a mile, then vanished from view in the grey mist.

Sarah's heart pounded in her body with fear and excitement. She walked slowly home thinking of the many things that had happened since the boy had arrived – Brendan's stammer cured, even if his father thought it was because of the money he had spent on therapy; the lake restored to its natural beauty; the wild creatures that came to him; Vaso's bird. So many lovely things – it was like a miracle.

As she climbed over the wooden fence which had barbed wire running through it, she remembered his leg that must have been torn. Yet that, too, was healed.

Her thoughts were shattered by the terrible noise of a chainsaw, the sound of which seemed to be coming from the wood. She ran there as fast as she could.

The sound grew louder and louder. Sarah's worst fears were realised. Several beautiful beech trees had been sent crashing to the ground, levelling the belts of rhododendrons.

A growing sense of panic and horror filled her as she passed the stumps of beech. There in the clearing she could see Joe tearing into her oak tree with his vile saw.

'Stop,' she yelled, as she clawed at his jacket, trying to pull him away from the tree.

'Are you crazy, you stupid little bitch,' yelled Joe. He tried to continue but she jumped on his back, her arms locked around his neck. Stopping the saw, he shook her off his back, sending her onto the ground.

'What are you playing at, Missie? I could have sawn you in half with this. It's bloody dangerous, what you did.'

'Leave my tree alone,' Sarah yelled, getting to her feet.

'Your tree, is it? Well, let me tell you I'm doing this for your old man.'

'I don't believe you, you weasel.'

Joe started up the saw again and continued to cut into the tree.

Sarah raced out of the woods, tears in her eyes. She saw her father working on the tractor.

'Dad, Dad,' she yelled, 'don't let him, please. Don't let him.'

Her father stood up wiping some oil from his hands with a cloth. 'What's the matter, Sarah?'

'Joe's cutting the oak tree. Please stop him.'

'Listen, young lady, I told him he could.'

'Please, Dad,' she pleaded, 'not that tree. He has already cut the five beech trees. Please, Dad, I beg you.'

Bill Robinson looked at her hard. How she resembled her late mother. Slowly he put out his left hand, wiped her tears and looked at the scar above her eye. Sarah looked into his sad eyes, which seemed lost in memory.

'Please, Dad,' she said softly. Her words seemed to jolt him. 'Okay, Sweetie, let's stop him.'

They ran across the fields until they reached Joe, who by now had made a deep gash in the tree. But it was still standing.

'Stop, Joe,' insisted Bill.

'I'll have it down in a couple of minutes.'

'I said stop,' roared Bill.

Joe stopped the saw. 'But you promised …'

Bill interrupted. 'I've changed my mind. You can sell the beech trees that we cut down, but no more. In fact, I don't want this wood touched ever again, except to plant a couple of beech trees.'

Joe looked at Bill as if he had lost his reason.

'Suit yourself, but I think you are being very foolish. Those trees are as good as hard cash.'

'No, Joe, they are better than hard cash.'

Joe pulled out a packet of cigarettes, put one in his mouth, forced a smile and lit up. 'Could do with a cup of tea, how about you, Bill?'

'Good idea.'

Joe walked ahead. Sarah hugged her father like she used to hug him when she was very small.

'Thanks, Dad,' she whispered, as more tears streamed down her face.

There was a lovely smell of apple tart as Sarah and her dad came through the kitchen door. Mary and Jamie were already tucking into their tea.

'I don't know what the world's coming to,' sighed Gran as she carried the hot tart to the table.

'What's the matter?' asked Bill, washing his hands in the kitchen sink.

'Oh, a dreadful thing has happened. I saw it on the six o'clock news, and when you think of all the shortages in the world ...'

Bill threw a look to heaven and sat down. 'Well, are you going to keep us in suspense all night or what?'

'There has been a terrible oil spill at sea, from one of those foreign tankers. Matt Whelan from the Fishery Board was interviewed. He says it's moving towards our coast. It seems the whole area will be ruined.'

'They showed other places where oil had killed thousands of sea birds and fish,' said Mary.

'Don't forget about the seals,' added Jamie.

Bill poured out his tea and cut some cheese.

'That's all we need, a disaster like that to ruin the livelihood of the fishermen and their families. Too many accidents like that nowadays. The Government will have to get tough on these people. We must watch the evening news and see how bad it is.'

Suddenly there was a knock on the back door, the latch lifted, and Joe entered. Sarah threw an angry glance at him.

'Evening, Bill, Mrs Robinson. Suppose you heard the news about the oil spill? Bet you're glad you're not a fisherman,' he said to Bill with a wry grin.

'We're all affected by a disaster like that,' replied Bill, annoyed.

'Oh, you're so right about that,' said Joe. 'It's terrible. That looks good,' he said noticing the tart.

'Sit yourself down,' said Gran, pouring him some tea and cutting him a slice.

'Don't suppose you have any ice cream in the freezer, Mrs Robinson?'

Gran took some ice cream from the fridge and pushed it towards him. Sarah watched him stuffing his face with the tart and ice cream, and swallowing big mouthfuls of tea. Pig, she thought.

'Did you hear about the lake over in the Tierney's place?' she said aloud.

'No,' said Bill.

'It's full of fish and ducks. Mike Tierney says you could nearly drink the water, it's so clean.'

'That's amazing,' said Bill. 'Sure that was supposed to be so polluted the local government insisted signs were to be put up and it had to be fenced off.'

'Isn't nature a wonderful thing?' said Gran. 'Thank God for a bit of good news.'

'Oh, it wasn't nature,' said Jamie. 'It was the boy, Rowan; he's got magic powers.'

Sarah coughed out her tea, spattering Joe on the arm.

'Sarah!' called her Dad, 'don't be so careless.'

'Are you all right, Joe?' said Gran.

Wiping his arm with his hankie, he remarked: 'It was a bit sweet,' then roared with laughter.

Bill broke into a loud laugh. Sarah glared at Jamie. Mary nudged him with her elbow.

'God, that was good,' said Joe, recovering from the laughter, 'even if I say so myself.'

Jamie's father looked at his son long and hard.

'Tell me more about the boy called Rowan. What did he do to the lake?'

Sarah answered for him. 'He's just a boy who arrived in the village one evening. We think he's an orphan.'

'He's lovely,' said Mary.

'He made us all hold hands around the lake and wish it better,' Jamie said.

'By God, that's a good one all right,' remarked Joe.

'*Wish* it better?' said Bill.

'He is a very gifted person with his hands and he's very good with animals,' said Sarah firmly.

'Indeed,' said her father. 'But no-one can make something better by wishing it better, now can they?'

'Don't forget how much old Tierney spent trying to clear that pollution and the time and the fish re-stocking he did.' Joe said.

'Yes, that's true,' said Bill. 'But did he not say it was a total failure, and that it was like pouring money down the drain.'

'Well,' said Gran, 'the main thing is it's all right again.'

'True,' said Bill, 'but I'm still curious about this mysterious young lad. Where does he live?'

There was no response from the children.

'I asked you a question. Where does he live?'

'In the barn,' said Mary.

'In whose barn?'

Looking at their faces, Bill gradually realised it was his barn they meant.

'I don't believe it. A young boy has been living in our barn and no-one told me about it?'

'Well, we were going to,' said Sarah nervously.

'When? Next year?' She could see her father was getting more annoyed by the minute.

'Well, it was a kind act,' insisted Gran, 'especially if he's an orphan. But you should have told your father at once.'

'Damn right they should have told me. Is he there now?'

'No,' said Sarah, 'he's gone away for a while, but he will be back.'

Joe suggested Bill should get on to the local police. They might know something about a missing boy.

'Don't let anyone hurt him, Dad, please,' said Mary. 'We all love him.'

Her father went quiet. Jamie added, 'Even Bingo loves him.'

'Well, that's good to hear,' said Bill, 'but I have to get to the bottom of this. I must know what's going on around here, do you all understand?'

'Quite right,' said Joe. 'A man has to be king in his own castle. Well, I'd better be off down to the local for a few scoops. I shouldn't worry too much about that young boy. I think the magic is in little Jamie's mind.'

*　　　*　　　*

When Joe was gone Gran suggested that the boy should come and stay with them.

'There's plenty of room. Besides, he seems a good influence on the children even though I've never laid eyes on him.'

Sarah, Mary and Jamie looked at their father with pleading faces.

A smile broke across his face. 'I suppose you're right, Gran. The weather is getting worse and I'd hate to think of one of my own living rough.'

'Does that mean he can live here?' asked Sarah.

'Yes, I guess so, for the time being. But no more intrigue behind my back. Is that clear, Sarah, and you two?'

Chapter 9

The moon illuminated the water. Captain Mercouri of the damaged vessel *Cormorant* stared out at the black oil which lay like tar on the surface of the sea. It would be daybreak before any attempt could be made to halt the spread of the vile liquid. At least the helicopters were gone.

The media are more interested in the story than in the problem, he thought to himself. Yet it was his fault, this devastation. How he hit those rocks he just couldn't explain. Admittedly, he had taken some whiskey to keep out the icy winds, but he wasn't drunk.

Now he would be ruined. He'd be remembered for having polluted one of the most beautiful coastlines in Europe, and not for the forty years of careful sailing in the most dangerous waters of the world. He thought of all the marine life that would be destroyed. It was like a nightmare.

As he watched, his eye caught a movement beyond the oil spillage, the silhouette of something gracefully, yet purposefully, moving around the black waters. Was it a dolphin? Yet, it seemed to have something on its back; it appeared luminous. He looked hard. It was like a boy.

Was it the moonlight playing tricks? He rubbed his tired eyes and tried to focus again. Watching the swells, he could see nothing. He grimaced, wishing he could awaken from this horror.

He was getting too old for this work, he thought. Yet he needn't worry now for he knew he would be finished when the news went worldwide.

Suddenly he saw the movement again; it definitely looked like a boy on a dolphin. Was he going mad? Was this a ghost or some sea spirit?

He could see them circling the waters. He couldn't call to anyone, for the crew had been taken to safety by helicopter. Captain Mercouri wanted to stay with his ship, come what may. He looked out into the blackness. There was nothing to see, and he felt so alone.

Then once again he glimpsed the dolphin and the boy. What was this vision? he wondered.

Suddenly, almost miraculously, the oil began to rise. Was it the wind? He tried to analyse what was happening before his eyes. If a storm blew up, the oil would spread even wider, causing more devastation.

He kissed the silver cross around his neck, then he saw a black wall of oil rise from the sea. Desperation turned to amazement. How could this happen? The oil was definitely rising. All around him the wall of black grew taller, tugging at the surface like some leech trying to hold onto its victim.

Then between the sea and the oil, a thin yellow light forced its way across the waves, and circled the entire area where the oil had spread.

This brilliant light wielded its power in a spectacle of splendour across the night sky, mingling through the black wall of the oil until a triumphant beam of yellow was all that could be seen. Captain Mercouri, too, felt enveloped by the radiant energies, as he watched the purification of the waters.

There was an afterglow of flame-coloured waves, and he watched them gently fade away. The waters looked calm and clear as the moonlight danced on the surface. There followed a hush and an atmosphere of complete peace.

In the distance he glimpsed a boy on a dolphin moving across the dark waves.

The Captain felt totally renewed as he watched the waters in peaceful reflection. He acknowledged to himself that he had experienced some supernatural event. No matter what might happen to him in the future he was very thankful that the sea was saved from this dreadful pollution.

The boy journeyed back towards the beach. He felt totally exhausted and chilled. As he got nearer he slipped from the dolphin, hugged him, and they parted. The dolphin moved swiftly out to the deep sea as the boy swam slowly towards the shore. When he reached the beach he staggered out of the water and collapsed on the sand.

*   *   *

Bill Robinson and the family waited anxiously for the evening news on the television. The whole village would be watching and waiting to see what was happening regarding the oil spillage.

The newscaster reported how the captain of the *Cormorant* had bravely stayed on his ship and, singlehanded, managed to suck the oil back into the containers, thus making it easy for the 'Operation Clean-up' ships to prevent any oil from spreading. The experts were baffled as to how the Greek captain had managed to avert the potential disaster. 'A friendly dolphin and a guardian angel helped me,' was all that Captain Mercouri would say.

There were messages of congratulation from the Prime Minister and many Council members.

The Greek Government also sent a message of praise to the sixty-year-old captain and promised him a hero's welcome on his return home.

'Well, could you credit that?' said Bill Robinson, 'isn't that wonderful!'

'Thank God,' said Gran. 'The fishermen and their wives

will sleep well tonight. Sarah,' she added, 'would you make a pot of tea, like a good girl.' Sarah looked at Jamie and Mary. 'Off to bed, you two,' added Gran.

'Night, Dad. Goodnight, Gran,' they said.

As they reached the stairs Sarah whispered to them: 'That was Rowan. He did it with his dolphin friend.'

'We knew that,' said Jamie.

'I hope he is all right,' said Mary.

'Of course he is,' said Sarah. 'Goodnight.'

Sarah went into the kitchen and put on the kettle. She whispered a quiet prayer for the boy, hoping he would be safe. If he was an angel, was it silly to say a prayer for him she wondered.

Then she remembered him mentioning pain before. Would someone like that feel more pain or less pain than a human? After she had made some sandwiches and tea she carried the tray into the sitting room.

'Dad, can I ask you something?'

'Yes, of course,' he replied, as he put down the paper. Gran was darning some socks and looking at the television.

'Would Jesus, who was human and divine, feel less pain or more pain than someone else who was just an ordinary person?'

'By God, that's one for the books,' replied her dad. 'What's all this religious talk all of a sudden?'

'I was just wondering, that's all,' came her reply.

'Well, that's a question for Fr Sheppard.'

Sarah poured the tea, but her dad could see how disappointed she was by his response. He picked up a sandwich, then answered: 'I suppose someone like the good Lord, or saints and holy people, would be finely tuned, like a violin or a harp, and so be more sensitive to things. Yes, I think they probably would feel joy or pain a whole lot more than we do.'

'I think I missed my vocation,' he continued to Gran. 'I should have been a priest or a preacher. What do you think?'

'I think you should stick to what you know best.'

This made Sarah's father smile. 'Oh, Mam, you haven't lost that sharp tongue, that's for sure.'

Then Gran looked over her glasses at Sarah: 'Remember, young lady, as my brother who was a priest, Lord rest his soul, once said, "We are all one hundred per cent human and one hundred per cent divine".'

Bingo barked; then there was a knock on the kitchen door.

'I'll go,' said Sarah, jumping up from the sofa. When she opened the door there stood Vaso, Kicker and Hammer, holding the boy by the arms. He looked so pale and weak.

'Quickly, take him over to the barn,' she said. ' I'll bring some clothes and food.'

Sarah hurried upstairs and collected his clothes. As she was coming down she met her father.

'Who is at the door at this hour, Sarah?'

'Vincent O'Brien, David Walsh, Peter Brown,' she swallowed hard … 'and Rowan.'

'Rowan! That's the young orphan boy?'

'Yes,' replied Sarah.

'Where is he?'

'In the barn,' said Sarah nervously.

'Well, bring him into the house.'

Chapter 10

'So this is Rowan?' enquired Bill Robinson. They shook hands.

Despite the boy's frail appearance, Bill Robinson could feel a warmth from his hand.

'Sarah, bring Rowan over to the fire. He looks frozen,' insisted her father. 'Gran, this is Rowan.'

'How are you?' asked Gran. 'Are you hungry?'

Without waiting for his reply she headed to the kitchen. The boy sat beside the warm fire and Bingo sat close to him. Bill Robinson sat across from the boy and looked at him for a long time without speaking.

Sarah moved awkwardly towards the sofa. There was a long silence.

Gran prepared some toast and raspberry jam and cut some of her boiled cake. She brought the tray in and placed it beside the boy.

'Eat up, young fellow, and tell us all about yourself.'

The boy smiled and took some toast. 'Are you from these parts?'

'No,' he replied.

'Is your family alive?' asked Bill Robinson.

Looking at Sarah, the boy then spoke. 'I suppose you would consider my family as passed over.'

'I understand, young fellow,' said Bill, with a tinge of sadness in his voice. 'My own wife, the Lord be good to her, has also passed away. Sarah there is so like her.'

'There is no death really,' said the boy. 'People move from one existence to another, that's all. Afterwards, they grow in love and understanding.'

'That's a lovely thought, Rowan. You're a wise young fellow for your age,' said Bill.

Then he added, 'You have been living in our barn. Have you no home?'

'I left my home to see what it was really like here.'

'Well, you can stay here as long as you like,' said Bill. 'You seem to have become part of the family, according to Jamie.'

'Have you brothers and sisters?' asked Gran.

'I consider everyone to be my brother and sister.'

Bill laughed at the boy's statement. 'Well, that's a great philosophy, young fellow. It should take you far.'

'If you've finished your supper, Rowan, Sarah will show you to your room,' said Gran.

'Thank you for your kindness.'

As he left, Gran remarked: 'A lovely lad, looks like he could do with a good meal.'

'Yes, he does seem remarkable,' replied Bill. Then, turning to Gran, he asked if she had been using an air freshener.

'An air freshener? What do you mean?'

'Well, there's a lovely delicate fragrance of wild flowers here.'

'Yes, there is a certain scent – probably those young ones being in and out through the wood.'

'Yes, perhaps you're right,' said Bill. 'Anyway, I'm off for a quick one.'

Turning to his mother, he said quietly, 'There is definitely something unusual about that young lad. I can sense it.' Then he left by the back door.

Gran, when she knew the boy had gone to bed, questioned Sarah about him.

Sarah related most of the things that had happened since meeting Rowan. Then Gran told her to go on up to bed.

There was something not quite of this world about the young boy, thought Gran, when Sarah had gone. He seemed friendly and kind and, if the stories were true, he certainly had remarkable gifts, but why come to their house? Taking a bottle of Lourdes water, which she had got from Sarah's mother, from the mantelpiece, she held it tightly in her hands, poured some into a glass, then filled it up with tap water.

Carefully, she walked up the stairs with the glass of

water. Knocking gently on the boy's door, she slowly pushed it open. For a moment she was dazzled by a beautiful rainbow light that filled the room. She stepped back nervously, then, looking again, all she saw was the bedroom light and the boy kneeling down.

'Oh, I hope I'm not disturbing you,' she said softly, 'but I thought you might like a little drink of water before you settle down for the night.'

'Thank you, that's just what I need after all the salt water.' The old woman looked puzzled. The boy slowly put the glass to his lips and sipped. He threw a glance at the old woman, then finished the water.

'Thank you, that was refreshing,' he said, handing her the glass. As she reached for it, he gently took hold of both her hands. She felt a surge of comforting energy flow through her arthritic joints. Her gnarled fingers, which had felt so much pain over the years, were now suddenly free of aches and their twisted form disappeared. She lifted her hands to her eyes and slowly moved each of her fingers. The feeling was wonderful.

With tears in her eyes, she embraced the boy and whispered a 'thank you' in his ear. Then she left.

Calling in to Sarah's room she hugged her. Sarah was surprised and comforted by the warm embrace. 'Only good comes from good,' Gran said in a thoughtful voice, and Sarah realised that Gran, too, had discovered how precious the boy was to their lives.

Chapter 11

Sarah awoke to the song of the birds. They were on the window sill and on the roof. She quickly washed, dressed and knocked on the boy's door. He was sitting by the window gently singing. There were birds on his shoulders and head and some on his hands, which he held out like a cup.

'Good morning,' said Sarah softly. The birds chirped about, then flew out the window and across the fields.

'Oh, I scared them,' said Sarah.

'No, they are hungry,' replied the boy. 'They are heading off to the woods and fields to find food.'

'Well, I'm hungry too. How about some breakfast?'

'Great,' he replied. 'I will be down to join you in a few minutes.'

It wasn't long before Sarah's father arrived in for breakfast with Joe.

Gran, Mary and Jamie joined them. Joe was about to

crack open his egg when the boy offered to say grace. Joe threw a glance at Bill and looked up to heaven.

Gran remarked that grace hadn't been said in the house since the death of Sarah's mother.

Joe reluctantly put down his bread knife and held an awkward pose as the boy, with eyes closed, whispered some words to himself. Then they began to eat.

'Who is this young fellow?' said Joe. 'Sarah's boyfriend?' He sniggered.

'He's a friend who's come to stay for a while,' said Jamie, sticking his tongue out at Joe.

After breakfast Bill remarked it was the nicest breakfast he had tasted in a long time.

'That's a good one,' said Gran. 'I've been giving you the same food for years. I haven't done anything different, but I will agree the bread was delicious.'

'A grand cup of tea too,' said Joe.

'You kids had better get yourselves ready for school,' urged Gran.

*   *   *

After breakfast, they set out for school. Sarah hoped the boy would be all right till she got back. She couldn't believe how well her father had taken to the situation and she could see he liked the boy. But Joe might prove difficult.

At school all the children asked about Rowan and spoke about the amazing things that had happened since his arrival. Vaso gave Sarah a present of a silver brooch with a picture of a dolphin on it.

'Thank you, Vaso, it's lovely.'

Embarrassed, he just shrugged his shoulders and said it was a 'memento'.

Betty and Gillian couldn't believe what they were seeing. But Sarah just smiled and went into the classroom.

* * *

All morning the boy worked, helping around the farm. He swept the farmyard, fed the hens and ducks and tidied up the shed where all the tools had been lying around.

Bill Robinson was delighted, as he never had time to get around to doing those small jobs. Gran watched with joy from the window at the boy giving Bingo a bath.

At about midday, the boy walked the dog over the fields towards the wood. As he approached, he could see two men taking away the beech trees. He hurried into the wood; there were ugly scars where the beech trees had stood.

On he moved towards the great oak, a knot of tension in his stomach. He could see how badly gashed the tree was, how deeply the saw had cut into its trunk. Walking around it, he surveyed the damage.

'Who would want to hurt such a majestic tree?' he whispered, tenderly moving his hands along the rough bark. Wiping a tear from his eye, he knelt down and held his hands a little away from the bark. He closed his eyes and waves of healing rays came from his palms, vibrating through the trunk. The oak quickly repaired itself with this powerful energy. The boy rested against the tree as a light rain began to fall. Bingo licked his hand and sat beside him.

＊　　　＊　　　＊

When Sarah arrived home, the boy was waiting for her at the fence.

'Come, I want to show you something,' he said in joyful tones.

Sarah was puzzled, but hurried after him as he ran across the fields. Jamie and Mary saw them running and chased after them. Bingo, too, followed behind. They did not stop running until they reached the wood.

Sarah suddenly looked at the boy.

'I know about the trees. It wasn't Dad's fault. It was Joe's idea.'

The boy put his fingers over her lips and took her by the hand. When they reached the oak tree Sarah couldn't believe her eyes.

'It's all right again!' she hugged the boy and then the tree. 'You can do anything,' she shouted out with joy.

'No, Sarah,' he said, 'I'm only a channel.'

They all made a circle with their hands and danced around the tree. Bingo jumped up, trying to join them, and they fell down on the soft leaves, laughing.

When they arrived back at the house the three Ryan sisters were waiting in the yard.

'Hello,' said Sarah. 'What do you want?'

The youngest, named Susan, replied: 'Can Rowan help make Philip better?'

'He's been sick for a long time now,' said the other sister, Jean.

'He's in a coma,' said Linda, the eldest.

'Well, I don't know. He's just going to have dinner,' said Sarah, speaking on the boy's behalf. 'Call back tomorrow.'

The girls looked disappointed. Rowan asked them what had happened to Philip.

Jean spoke up. 'He was delivering newspapers and when he got to Williams's house …'

'Mr Williams sells cars,' interrupted Linda.

'I'm telling it,' said Jean. 'Well, he was putting the paper through the letterbox when the dog jumped over the back fence and attacked him.'

'It was a Rottweiler,' said Linda.

Jean continued: 'He got a terrible shock. Luckily, Mr Williams came out in time to stop the dog from biting him badly, but the doctors think he may have hit his head when he fell.'

'That's terrible, where is he now?'

'In the County Hospital, St Gabriel's. He's been like that for months,' said Linda.

'I will go and see him, I promise.'

The sisters looked pleased. They thanked him and

hurried away. Sarah ran after them.

'Rowan will do the best he can, but you mustn't tell anybody just yet. We'll have to wait and see.'

'Okay, Sarah,' they answered and ran down the drive.

The boy asked where the hospital was. Sarah told him, and he started off immediately.

'Wait till after dinner,' insisted Sarah.

'Please tell your Gran I will be back later.'

'Can I go with you?'

'No. I'd better go alone.'

'Let's have some dinner, I'm starving,' said Jamie.

Then the boy departed.

*　　　*　　　*

Walking through the village, the boy looked at the rows of houses where the families lived, all sharing their different lives inside four walls. Some had children, other people lived alone. Some were born in those houses; others would pass away in them – all linked together in the great mystery of life, each one precious and unique.

He would have liked to knock on each door to tell them they were all precious jewels shaped by creation, and that they should allow themselves to sparkle, to be aware of life's true meaning.

Living is an art, he would tell them. Each person's contribution is uniquely valuable and necessary. However dim the spark, the fire of creativity can be kindled, revealing their true nature. Then a new lustre of achievement can be obtained. No longer need lives be inhibited by the darkness of exploitation and fear. When will man be ready for this revelation? he wondered, as he passed by.

The lights were on in the grounds of the hospital. He looked at the empty flower beds, which awaited spring, the tall cypress trees, floodlit on either side. Reaching the splendidly carved entrance, he pressed the brass bell.

Several moments later, a rather cross-looking nurse stared down at the boy who stood waiting on the granite steps.

'Can I help you?' she asked, sounding annoyed.

'May I come in and see someone?' the boy replied politely.

'Visiting hours are from three to four, and six-thirty to eight o'clock.' Then she slammed the heavy door shut.

The boy walked down the steps, then circled the granite building. Looking up, he could see a beautiful carving of the Angel Gabriel with outstretched hands. Noticing several windows partially open, he decided to climb the drainpipe.

It proved extremely difficult, but the building was partially covered with Virginia creeper which made it a little easier.

Finally he reached the roof. He walked along the ornate top then, carefully lowering himself onto a window ledge, climbed in a window.

There were two empty beds in the dimly-lit room. He

left that room quickly and walked lightly down a corridor. Hearing footsteps, he hid in another room. A nurse walked up with some orange juice on a tray.

'Now, Major,' she said to the frail old man lying in the bed, 'here's your drink.'

'Nurse, put the other light on, will you?'

'Certainly. I'll look in later, Major.'

As she left the room, the young woman met a fellow-nurse.

'Poor old Major, he's still having those nightmares of his war days.'

'It's a shame at eighty-three to be afraid of the dark,' remarked the other nurse.

'It's afraid to die he is. He feels very guilty about his involvement in the war, blames himself for those dead people. He told me that he used to be so proud of his achievements, yet now he looks back with horror. There's no telling him that it happened such a long time ago and that so many other people went through the same horrors. It must be hard on him all the same. Never having experienced a war situation, I wouldn't know what it was like.'

'Thank God we didn't,' said the other nurse. 'Normal life is enough for me to handle.'

'The Vicar calls regularly to the Major. He has great talks with him, and I know it helps. But it's in the evening time that he gets most troubled.'

'Has he no family?' asked the other nurse.

'Not that I know of. Poor old fellow, it's no joke

breaking a hip at his age.'

The Major finished his juice and was about to put on the radio when he suddenly sensed a presence in the room and a fragrance of flowers. Waves of light began to move around.

The Major tried to reach for the nurse's bell, yet he didn't feel that awful panic of previous nights.

Turquoise-blue beams rose above his head, rimming the ceiling, then orange-yellow swells of colour appeared. As he looked into them he saw the beautiful, radiant face of a boy. As the moments passed, the old man became calm. He felt strengthened by the shafts of light that pierced through his body. In the light he briefly saw the tortured battlefields, then they vanished. The fields were now filled with wild flowers and young children running and playing.

'Is it time for me to go?' he asked.

Then the Major gently slipped into a joyous sleep ...

Elsewhere, a baby covered with ointment and bandages lay in a cot, crying in her sleep as she tried to scratch her inflamed skin. The boy leaned into the cot and removed the bandages. He slowly moved his hands over the little body. The baby became calm and slept soundly, and the red blotches on her skin disappeared.

The boy covered her with the cotton sheet, then slipped quietly away and down the stairs to the next level.

The first room off the corridor was where Philip Ryan lay. The boy peeped in and, looking behind him once, he entered the room.

A teddy bear lay tucked in beside Philip and several books were unopened on his locker. Football posters had been stuck above the bed and get-well cards hung over the metal bedhead. A drip was attached to Philip as he lay in suspended sleep.

The boy switched on the night light, then knelt down beside the bed and closed his eyes. From the clutches of liquid darkness that had seized his mind, Philip suddenly felt a release.

Floating through realms of murky clouds of grey that fogged his senses, he ascended higher to dream consciousness. A mauve half-light peeled away the grey that had enveloped him. He could feel a gentle breeze across his face, like he was being fanned by delicate wings. Smell, sight and hearing blossomed from his dream-consciousness into reality.

A brilliant light flared up in his mind, washing away any traces of the coma that had so ensnared his being. His eyes focused on a beautiful face. Blue eyes looked back at him. He could see the form of a boy standing at the end of the bed. A warm smile made Philip feel calm.

As he adjusted to his surroundings, he knew he wasn't in his own bedroom, but the posters, the books, and the teddy bear were his.

Forcing himself into an upright position, he looked for the boy, but he was gone. Then he became aware of the drip attached to his arm. With the other, he reached over for a glass and poured a drink of mineral water for himself.

At that very moment, his mother and father entered the room. They couldn't believe their eyes.

'Hi, Mum. Hi, Dad,' said Philip.

His parents rushed to embrace him, crying tears of joy.

*   *   *

The boy slipped quietly down the stairs, past all the visitors who were arriving and left by the front door. The Vicar had come to see the Major and was delighted to find him so contented and was surprised to discover how quickly the hip was mending. The Major asked the vicar of he would help him put his wartime experiences on tape. This pleased the vicar greatly as he had been trying to persuade the Major for a very long time to do this in the hope of writing it up some time.

In another part of the hospital, a mother clutched her little baby in a warm embrace, relieved to see that her skin had completely cleared. The baby pulled at her hair and tried to chew it.

*   *   *

As the boy walked through the village, he was greeted by Vaso, Kicker and Hammer. They were surprised and pleased to see him. They offered him some of the chips they had just bought.

The boy took one and then Vaso asked if he would like to see his racing pigeons. The boy nodded and they headed back to Vaso's home.

Brendan passed them on his bike. Vaso called to him and asked would he also like to see the 'racers'. Brendan was really chuffed – he had been included!

*   *   *

Sarah sat by the window, gazing down the driveway, awaiting the return of the boy. The rest of the family had eaten and were watching television. Gran had put Rowan's dinner in the oven, knowing he would be late back.

Then to her great delight, Sarah saw the boy walking up the drive, and hurried out to greet him.

Chapter 12

A heavy fog mantled the city, street lights forced their rays through the grey-white shield. Indistinct grey shapes appeared through the thick blanket of fog, as they hurried to their destinations. Cars and buses moved slowly, their yellow lights trying to pierce the fog's choking embrace.

A tall dark form, well-covered for the weather, ambled unconcernedly along the street, tapping the path with a silver-handled cane in time to his step. He had travelled far, but soon his journey would lead him to the place he knew the boy would be.

* * *

The next few days passed quietly. The boy was very helpful around the farm. Sarah's father was a lot happier within himself. The terrible nagging pains that had tortured his mind since the crash in which his lovely Janie lost her life were gone. He was now able to talk openly about it to his mother and Sarah, without pain or anger.

Gran enjoyed the boy's company and she seemed to have renewed energy since his arrival. The village children met with the boy each afternoon when school finished, in the wood or by the seashore.

Sarah was keeping a diary of everything that was happening. Philip Ryan's recovery was the talk of the village. He, too, came to visit the boy, realising it was he who had awakened him from the coma.

Sergeant Thorpe was the only one who seemed suspicious. He and Garda O'Connell had noticed a decline in petty crime in the area. The village had no serious crime problem, but had its fair share of petty misdemeanours. Even the teenage cider parties on the pier had ceased. Sergeant Thorpe should have been relieved, yet he had a policeman's mind – he would be the first to admit he was a sceptic.

One evening Gran sat knitting and listening to the radio. The dog lay snoozing on the rug. Bill Robinson threw another log on the fire, sending a brief shower of sparks up the chimney.

Sarah and the boy were finishing the washing-up after the evening meal.

'I have something for you,' he said casually, as he placed the last plate in the cupboard.

'Really?' said Sarah. 'What is it?'

'It's a surprise.'

'I love surprises,' she said excitedly. 'Can I see it?'

'Close your eyes and put out your hands. Keep them closed,' he insisted, as he took something from the drawer. 'Now, can you guess what it is? But keep your eyes closed.'

Sarah felt something being placed in her hands. It felt like wood, smooth and curved.

'Can you guess?' he asked.

'It's wood. Polished wood. Something carved?'

'Well done,' came the reply.

She opened her eyes and stared at the beautiful carved dolphin with a boy astride it.

'Oh, it's wonderful,' she exclaimed, as her fingers caressed the delicate carving. 'Where did you get it?'

He did not reply, only looked warmly at her.

'You didn't carve it, did you?'

He nodded. She threw her arms around him.

'It's lovely.'

'I wanted you to have something to remember me by.'

She looked puzzled. Then the phone rang, making Gran, who was beginning to doze in the armchair, jump.

Bill Robinson picked up the phone. 'Hello! Who? Oh, hello, Fr Sheppard.' He listened intently, while he turned to stare at the boy.

'Well, I suppose tomorrow night would suit okay. Yes. Goodnight to you.'

Putting down the phone, he slowly explained that the local committee wanted to come and visit Rowan the following night.

'I have no idea what it's all about, young man, but you'd better be here and ready for them. They're coming at eight.'

The boy didn't seem troubled, but Sarah was perturbed. It's hard to explain things to adults at times, she thought to herself.

Gran said nothing, but gave a knowing glance at the boy.

*   *   *

The following day Sarah was told off on several occasions by the teacher for not paying attention. Sarah apologised, but found it impossible to concentrate. Her mind raced with anxious thoughts about the evening's meeting.

Later, she tried to warn the boy to be careful and not to say anything that might disturb the committee, but the boy just smiled.

'Things will be fine. We all have to do what has to be done,' he added calmly.

*   *   *

At the stroke of eight, the committee arrived: Fr Sheppard; Fr Keating; Reverend Jones; Mary Stokes, the local councillor; Con Hughes, the librarian; Dr Simms and Sergeant Thorpe.

Bill Robinson welcomed them and brought them into the sitting-room. Gran had tea, coffee and biscuits ready.

'Oh, you shouldn't have gone to any trouble,' said Con

Hughes, who was the chairperson.

'No trouble,' said Gran cheerfully. 'He's a good child, so don't go upsetting him,' she added sharply, and left the room.

They glanced uncomfortably at each other.

'This is Rowan,' announced Bill. 'Do you want me to stay?' he asked the boy.

'No, thanks,' said the boy, 'I'll be fine.'

Sarah was not allowed into the room. She sat in the kitchen, nervously tapping her fingers on the pine table.

All eyes stared at the boy. They sat around him, each of them sensing something unusual about him. Councillor Stokes and Fr Keating held paper and pens in their hands.

Con Hughes spoke first: 'Rowan, you seem to have a great way with the local children; they all talk very highly of you. Why do you think that is?'

'Because they are my brothers and sisters.'

Hughes looked at the others. The councillor asked what age he was and where was he from.

'I'm twelve years old and I'm from the Celestial City.'

'The Celestial City?' said Fr Keating. 'Can you explain?'

'Where love and harmony spring from,' he replied.

'Is it true you have special powers?' asked Dr Simms.

'We all have special powers,' said the boy. 'The greatest is love. It is the life-blood of the planet. Our well-being depends on it. It's the rhythm of life. It must be realised in our hearts, then we can send it out. Darkness will give way to love's revealing light.'

They were astonished at his answers.

'How does one express this love you speak about?' asked the Reverend Jones.

'By giving,' said the boy, 'whether it's food, clothing, money, friendship or understanding. These are the things that begin the flow. Everyone benefits from a good deed, just as everyone suffers from a bad one. Across the planet millions starve and die. Countless others survive in misery and hopeless poverty, condemned to suffer from birth to death. This is because the concept of sharing is alien to man's thinking. He looks with suspicion on such ideas.'

The boy continued: 'Sharing is the natural order of things. Selfishness and greed are departures from the norm, causing sorrow and separation. The wise see the need for sharing as the only basis of lasting peace. We must be ready to act in the spirit of brotherhood and love.'

'You are very wise for your age, young man. How did you acquire such knowledge and wisdom?' asked Fr Sheppard.

'The bird sings, not because it has a message, but because it has a song,' replied the boy.

'Is there such a thing as evil?' said Sergeant Thorpe.

'The brighter the light, the darker the shadow,' came the reply.

Con Hughes spoke: 'There are so many troubles in the world, and most people live in fear and dread of these things. What would one say of them?'

'There are many obstacles on our journey through life.

None hinders more than fear – fear of failure, fear of pain, fear of ridicule, fear of discipline, of suffering. Fear obstructs the flow of life itself. It takes away hope and torments one with doubt and despair. Again, I say to you all, sharing will bring peace and love, and will banish fear.'

'What is your understanding of God?' asked Fr Keating.

The boy closed his eyes and spoke: 'God is the Divine Composer and Celestial Musician, composing and performing. His creative symphony has many beautiful variations. He is the Divine Dancer. He determines the movements of the planets, the flow of river, waterfall and stream, the movement of the waves, the swaying of trees and flowers, the flight of birds. He is the Sacred Weaver whose many-coloured tapestry is woven on the loom of time and space.'

'How beautiful,' exclaimed the local councillor.

'What about all those who set out to hurt and destroy?' asked Con Hughes.

'Those who sow the wind, reap the whirlwind.'

Dr Simms then asked: 'How do you feel about what's happening to the planet?'

'The Earth is a living entity, complete in all its parts, each essential to the whole. A halt must be called to this unholy war on nature. A new vision and new sanity must prevail. Many are realising this and are becoming true custodians of the planet. Man has the power to enhance or to destroy his world.'

'Why do you think people are born?' asked the Reverend Jones.

'To integrate the planet. It's a training ground for the mind and soul. After all, we are only guests in this planet – we must not hurt or destroy her.' Then he added quietly: 'However he may try, man cannot live without love.'

The committee was reduced to silence. They had all experienced a warm glow from the boy's presence and his words touched them all deeply.

They decided to leave. They each shook his hand and thanked him.

'One little thing,' asked Fr Sheppard. 'There is a fund-raiser for the school tomorrow night. We hope to have as many families as possible there. We hear you're a lovely singer. Is there any chance you could take part in the concert? Perhaps you could sing a song or two?'

'I would be honoured,' said the boy.

Sarah and her father were relieved that everything went well with Rowan and the committee members.

'You really have become part of our family,' said Bill Robinson.

'Thank you,' said the boy, and he headed off to bed.

Chapter 13

'Have you got your recorder?' called Bill Robinson from the bottom of the stairs.

'Yes, Dad,' replied Jamie as he slid down the banisters.

'Good. Are you ready, Gran?' he asked, looking at Mrs Robinson who was putting on her hat.

'Don't rush me; I'll be ready in a moment.'

'This is very exciting,' said Sarah. 'Jamie playing the recorder, Mary in the school choir and you singing solo.'

'It's a pity you are not playing the piano,' said the boy.

'Oh, I'm very rusty, out of practice. Gillian will be much better; she's very talented.'

They all got into the car and headed for the Town Hall.

* * *

The hall was packed to capacity. Con Hughes was the compere. He told a few jokes to warm up the audience

– not that he had to, for there was great excitement among the schoolchildren.

The parents watched proudly as their children performed. Gillian got loud applause for her playing of Beethoven's 'Für Elise'. Jamie played 'Greensleeves', stopping only twice during the piece.

Bill Robinson beamed with pride and nudged Gran, who was nodding off because of the heat, as Mary and the choir began a medley of songs from popular musicals.

After the interval the raffle was held, the school brass band played, and got a rousing response from the audience. Then Con Hughes came out and thanked the band.

'My next performer is a remarkable young fellow, who is on a visit to our village, and staying with the Robinsons. I met him for the first time last evening. I'm told he sings even better than me.'

This brought shrieks, jeers and whistles.

'Please put your hands together and give a big welcome to our guest singer, Rowan Bird, who is going to sing, "The Song of Creation".'

The children clapped loudly. Sarah shifted in her seat and chewed at her fingers. She felt more nervous than if she had to sing herself.

The boy walked out slowly from behind the curtain and moved towards the microphone. He could not really see the audience because of the two spotlights, focused on the stage. He closed his eyes and began to sing.

He sang with such creative joy, his rich melodic voice

rising and falling like a gentle breeze or a babbling brook, that the audience was captivated. Tears streamed down Fr Sheppard's face. Rowan's voice, he felt, was a pure channel, each note sung in perfect harmony.

When he had finished, everyone felt uplifted and inspired. The song seemed to go beyond hearing, touching everyone's very heart and soul.

Con Hughes clicked his camera at the boy from the wings. The audience clapped loudly and whistled in appreciation.

The boy walked slowly off the stage. The audience called for more, but he didn't come back on.

Con Hughes reminded people it was getting late, told some more jokes, thanked the children for performing, and the organisers. Finally, he thanked the audience for making the evening such a success.

As the last notes of the National Anthem sounded, a tall, dark stranger slid in through the doorway. His piercing eyes scanned the hall and finally settled on the boy, who was surrounded now by children. The stranger leaned against the wall and slowly unscrewed the top of his walking stick, revealing it to be a sword cane. Pulling the blade halfway out, he moved towards the boy. The crowded auditorium, and the people pushing towards the main exit blocked his progress.

Bill Robinson put one arm around Rowan and the other around Sarah.

'C'mon you two. Well done, young man, that was

beautiful.' The boy looked pleased, and smiled at Sarah. Jamie and Mary held Gran's hand.

'Can we buy chips, Dad, please?' asked Jamie.

'Oh, very well,' said Bill Robinson as they reached the foyer, and made their way outside into the cold night air.

Inside the auditorium Con Hughes was on the stage. As he began to disconnect the speakers, the dark stranger clamped a hand on his shoulder.

'May I have a word?'

*　　　*　　　*

When they arrived home, Gran announced she was fit only for bed. Jamie and Mary were delighted that there was no school the following day and slowly made their way upstairs.

'I'm turning in too,' said Sarah's father. 'Some people have to work in the morning.' He smiled at Sarah and the boy.

'Don't stay up late, you two.'

'No, Dad,' said Sarah.

'Goodnight, Mr Robinson.'

'Goodnight, you two, sleep well.'

'Would you like some supper, Rowan?' asked Sarah.

'No thanks, not after all those chips. A glass of water would be lovely, though.'

Sarah went to the kitchen and got the water. As she passed it to him, she looked deeply into his eyes.

'You sang like an angel,' she said softly, choosing her words carefully.

'Thank you,' he replied, then slowly drank the water.

'Did you ever sing here before?' asked Sarah.

'Once,' he said quietly, his eyes recalling the time. He beamed a beautiful smile.

'When?' insisted Sarah, 'and where?'

'Well, it was far away from here, on a cold, starry night, a long, long time ago.' He touched her face.

'Goodnight. Sleep in heavenly peace,' he said, as he walked towards the stairs.

'Sleep in heavenly peace,' repeated Sarah to herself. She had heard those words before. But where? Then she remembered. They were from the Christmas carol 'Silent Night'! But that was written about a hundred years ago! What is he trying to tell me? she wondered. Oh my God! Is he trying to tell me he was one of the angels singing on that very first Christmas?! My God, no one will believe this. He really *is* an angel!

Somehow she had known it all along. However, now that he had more or less come out and admitted it, the realisation made her tremble. She walked up the stairs, paused at his door, then went into her bedroom and collapsed on the bed in amazement.

She ran her hands through her hair. An angel! My God, an angel! This is incredible.

She wanted to rush out and tell everyone. She smiled and grabbed one of her dolls. 'Do you know there is an angel sleeping next door? I'm so lucky, so privileged,' she said.

She slumped back on the bed. And I have seen him … touched him.

Then she sat upright. If people find out they might hurt him. I'd better not say anything, just let things proceed as they are. This is fantastic!

*   *   *

All night a dolphin moved fearfully through the dark waters of the harbour.

Chapter 14

The boy drummed his fingers nervously on the pine table, as he glanced out at the early-morning light, then he rose and paced to the window, where he stood staring across the fields. The rooks were feeding in the garden.

A robin alighted on the window sill and bobbed about. The boy emptied some crumbs from the bread-board into his palm and walked back to the window. He gently opened it and the robin jumped onto his hand. A chaffinch soon joined it, then a dunnock. When they had eaten the crumbs, the boy closed the window and re-seated himself at the table.

Sarah came in. For a moment the boy didn't see her. He was still staring out the window.

'A penny for them?' said Sarah.

The boy looked at her and smiled. 'Good morning.'

Sarah sat beside him, looked him in the eye and said

gently. 'Did you mean what you said last night?'

'Yes,' he said. She hugged him tightly.

'My God, we're so lucky just having you around us.'

'There are many more,' said the boy. 'All there to help and serve.'

'Can I ask you something? Why did you not appear to someone more important than me? And why appear in a village? Why not in a big city, get on television and in the newspapers?'

He smiled and said: 'No one is more important than anyone else in spirit. In big cities people are too distracted. Besides, I came specially to see you.'

Sarah was astonished. 'Me?'

'I can't explain, but you will just have to believe me. I may not be around much longer.'

'Why not?' she asked sadly.

'I'm not sure. I sense that something is about to happen. But I will always hold you in my heart and thoughts.'

Sarah was about to question him further when Gran walked in.

'Good morning. Is the kettle on? I'm in a bad way for a cuppa.'

Sarah took the kettle, filled it with water, then she left with Rowan.

Bill Robinson arrived in from the fields for breakfast. As he was eating, the phone rang.

'It's for you, Dad,' shouted Jamie.

'Hello?' said Bill. 'Oh, hello, Con. Yes, I enjoyed the

evening very much.'

Gran saw the expression change on her son's face. Then he said: 'You mean this morning? Well, I suppose so, if it's that urgent. Eleven o'clock in councillor Stokes's office. Right, see you there.' Putting down the phone, he went back to the table.

'What is it?' Gran asked.

After a long pause, he told her that the committee wanted to see him urgently, that a certain Dr Ahriman had come to collect the boy.

'Oh dear,' sighed Gran. 'We'll miss him terribly.'

Putting on his coat and hat, he added: 'I'd better see what all this is about. Where are Sarah and Rowan?'

'I think they've gone to the wood, Dad,' said Jamie.

'Well, nobody say anything about this until I get back.' Then he left by the kitchen door.

'Hey, Joe,' shouted Bill, 'I have to head into the village. Keep an eye on things till I get back.'

'Okay, Bill, see you later.'

*　　　*　　　*

The atmosphere in the conference room seemed tense as Bill Robinson entered. The committee members were seated around a large table. Bill's eyes were immediately riveted to the stranger sitting at one end.

Con Hughes awkwardly introduced Bill Robinson to Dr Ahriman. The tall, dark-haired man stood, extended his hand, and Bill Robinson took hold of it.

They stared hard at each other. The smile across the carved features of Dr Ahriman seemed hollow. Bill Robinson distrusted him immediately.

Coffee and biscuits were brought, then Con Hughes began. 'It seems that the young boy who is staying in your house, Bill, escaped from a Psychic Research Institute run by Dr Ahriman here, and somehow managed to stow away on a ship and ended up in our village.'

'Maybe I should explain,' said Dr Ahriman. 'The boy in question is a most remarkable young person. He has been the subject of a secret project, and has been highly programmed in the sciences and the arts. All the great philosophies and religions were being taught to him. We were training his mind and body to the highest standards. As you witnessed last evening, even his voice has been worked on. Have you ever heard a finer singer?'

Fr Sheppard shook his head.

'The problem is that the boy has been brought up in an institution. He knows no mother or father, only the people who work with him.'

'It sounds very cold and soulless,' remarked Reverend Jones.

'Well, my dear Reverend, "soul" is not the language of scientists. It was I who gave him the grounding in philosophy and religion. It's so important to have an overview, even if we are all an accident of evolution. Please forgive me. I do beg your pardon, gentlemen of the cloth, I don't wish to offend by that flippant remark.'

'The children say he has magical powers,' said Con Hughes.

'Children are full of magic,' answered Dr Ahriman. 'But it's true. He does have extraordinary psychic powers. He has developed the gift of telekinesis. He can move things around on a table, even bend spoons.'

'We all had conversations with him,' remarked Fr Keating. 'He seems far more special than someone who has simply mastered some psychic powers. His wisdom is so pure and clear.'

'Oh, I agree with you. He is our pride and joy, but let me ask you something. Has he said anything new to you that you have not read or heard before?'

The councillor, Mary Stokes, said self-consciously: 'My two children have spent a lot of time with him, and they think he's an angel.'

Dr Ahriman broke into loud laughter. 'Oh, forgive me,' he said, trying to stifle his mirth, 'I do agree he has a charismatic personality, but he has been taught and trained to develop that quality and, I may add, no money has been spared in his education.'

'With all due respect, Dr Ahriman, how do we know what you are saying is true?' asked Bill Robinson.

'I appreciate your concern. Here are my references.' He pulled out a black folder with numerous degrees and references attached.

'Most impressive,' said Dr Simms, as he flicked through the pages.

'Why can't the boy stay with us?' asked Bill Robinson. 'He seems happy. We'll give him a good home and he's got plenty of company.'

'A kind gesture, indeed,' said Dr Ahriman, 'but I haven't told you the real problem. You see, the boy has a rare blood type. He must be kept under our protection, otherwise he will die. I can't stress this strongly enough.'

'He seems perfectly normal to me,' insisted Bill.

'Seems normal, yes,' said Dr Ahriman. 'However, if you don't believe me, get Dr Simms to take a blood sample.'

'That sounds fair enough,' said Dr Simms.

'I suppose so,' said Bill.

'My only worry is he might try and escape again and, if he does, it might prove fatal to him,' added Dr Ahriman.

*   *   *

The young people gathered in the wood with the boy, unaware of what was happening in the village. Whenever the boy spoke, he had a remarkable way of conveying more than words. While talking very simply, he would seem to convey an awareness of what lay behind the words. So often in his conversations it would seem that his real purpose was, first of all, to give. He would not try to persuade anyone to follow a line of thought and seemed to have little concern with mental arguments.

Above all, he wanted to bring a quality of love to the heart of the listener. He spoke of light and harmony pouring into the world to heal and cleanse the planet.

One of the children asked him to describe the earth from his viewpoint.

'It is that beautiful sphere shining blue and silver in the velvet sea of space, turning, according to divine law, though the depths of the heavens.'

A girl asked him about Jesus.

'I cannot adequately paint in words a picture of His glory, His gentle and gracious spirit. He lived to heal, to comfort and to illumine. His mission was to prepare the world for Divine love. He came as a shaft of light from the heavens, and anchored that love by the wooden cross, flooding the whole world with His Christ-light. Light-bearers continue their outpouring of love to this precious planet.'

'What about you?' asked another. 'Is that why you are here?'

The boy smiled. 'I'm just a visitor, a humble servant come to learn and discover a little more about the great mystery called Life.'

'You seem to understand a great deal more than we do,' said Gillian.

*   *   *

Suddenly they heard heavy footsteps. Brendan crashed through the undergrowth. He was panting hard, and barely able to speak.

'What is it?' asked Sarah.

'The police... and some adults ... on their way ... to

get Rowan. I heard them myself. They were talking ...
outside the police station to Sergeant Thorpe, Fr Sheppard, Reverend Jones and Con Hughes. There were lots
of them ... oh! and some stranger who wants to take you
away.'

'We must hide you,' said Sarah, 'but where?'

Vaso shouted from the crowd 'I know ... Raven's View.
Near the old quarry.'

'Yes, that's a great idea. Quick, we must hurry.'

Joe was out with his shotgun when he saw the children
running out of the woods.

Now where are they off to? he wondered. They sure
seem in a hurry.

Several cars arrived at Robinson's farm. The police
were first. Bill Robinson arrived next and hurried into the
house.

'Have Sarah and the boy arrived back?'

'No,' said Gran. 'Good heavens, what are the police
doing here?' By this time, several cars had come up the
drive.

'We will have to go on foot from here,' said Bill.

'What's going on?' asked Gran.

'I'll tell you later. We're in a hurry. Where are Jamie and
Mary?'

'In the wood with Sarah and Rowan.'

'Oh God!' said Bill, slamming the door behind him. 'Joe,
Joe!' he shouted, as they hurried up the fields.

Joe looked a little embarrassed with the shotgun in his

hand. 'It's those blasted rats, at the grain again.'

'Never mind that now,' said Bill, interrupting him. 'Did you see Sarah and Rowan?'

'I saw the whole lot of them heading up the slopes. They seemed to be making for the old quarry.'

*　　　*　　　*

Raven's View was a steep ridge. Below it was a sandy cove; to the side was the old rock quarry. Fulmars hung on the wind as the children hurried to the top. The wind blew strong and cold. They could hear the pounding of the waves below and feel the salt spray on their faces. The sheep scattered as they drew near.

'Stop, you lot,' shouted a voice from below. They looked back to see about twenty adults making their way up the slopes.

Garda O'Connell, holding a police dog, yelled again. 'Stop!'

'What will we do?' said Brendan. 'We're trapped.'

'I don't know,' said Sarah, staring back at her father and Joe, who were nearly upon them.

'Listen, everybody,' said Sergeant Thorpe, trying to get his breath. 'This gentleman has come to collect the boy. Now, where is he?'

Sarah looked at Dr Ahriman. She didn't like his cold stare.

'We don't want to hurt him,' said Dr Simms.

'You want to take him away,' yelled Sarah.

'Where is he?' demanded her father.

Sarah looked behind her. The boy wasn't with the others, yet he had been a minute ago.

'Hey, look over the ridge,' yelled Joe.

The boy and Vaso were climbing down the steep cliff.

'Quick,' said Vaso to the boy. 'We can jump to the sand after the next bit.'

'You lot stay here,' said Sergeant Thorpe to the children, as he and the other adults hurried to the edge.

'Stop them,' shouted Dr Ahriman.

'A little further,' yelled Vaso, 'then we can jump.'

Sarah started to climb down the far side when the others weren't looking. Joe looked over, fingering his shotgun. Dr Ahriman stared down as the boy jumped to the sand.

'We made it,' said Vaso.

Dr Ahriman gazed hard at Joe, making direct eye contact. Joe trembled, then raising the shotgun to his shoulder, he leaned over the cliff, aimed at the boy and let go with both barrels.

The deafening sound pierced the air. Sarah nearly fell off the cliff with fright, then she looked down and saw Vaso screaming loudly: 'He's been shot. My God, he's been shot.'

The boy lay face down. Sarah threw herself off the ridge and crashed onto the sand. She crawled over to him.

'Oh no! This is terrible. Get help.'

Vaso climbed back towards the top, the policeman pulling him up the final stretch.

'We'd better phone for an ambulance,' said Dr Simms.

Bill Robinson lunged at Joe. 'What the hell did you do that for?'

Sergeant Thorpe pulled him away.

Joe, panting, yelled back: 'It went off by accident. I didn't mean it ... It was Dr what's-his-name ... Ask him.'

'Where is he?' said Reverend Jones. They looked all around, but Dr Ahriman was nowhere to be seen.

All the children were crying, as Sarah cradled the boy tenderly in her arms. She could feel blood running down his back. What a terrible way for things to end, she thought.

'Dear Sarah, don't despair, remember our real selves can never be hurt, or wounded, or die. Please believe me ... promise?'

Tears dropped from her face onto his. He touched her forehead.

'This is my last gift to you.'

She didn't understand what he meant. Then he asked her to help him to the sea.

'Let us bring you to hospital,' she pleaded.

'No, Sarah. This is the way it must be.'

'Sarah,' shouted her father, as he watched her help the boy into the water, walking in with him up to her shoulders.

'What now?' she asked the boy.

'Now we must part. Tell them I love them all very dearly and I will remember them always, and especially you.'

She held him tightly. His body felt limp. Then he smiled.

'Tell the librarian to look below the kneeling flagstone at St. Colman's Well ...'

Sarah felt something brush her back. She turned to see a dolphin. It nuzzled her. She helped the boy onto its back. He lay silently, then reached out and held her hand gently.

The dolphin moved slowly away. Sarah watched as they seemed to blend with the waves. Then they were gone ...

By now, the whole crowd had climbed down to the beach. There was silence.

Sarah's father put his arm around her. 'I'm sorry, love, really sorry. Come on, we'll get you home and out of those wet clothes.'

Sarah smiled a sad smile.

'He's not really dead,' said Jamie. 'You can't kill an angel.'

Bill Robinson gathered his children to him, and together they walked silently home.

Epilogue

The community became more united as a result of these events. Their hearts and minds had been touched deeply by their brief encounter with the boy.

Con Hughes put the village on the map by discovering an illuminated manuscript at St Colman's Well. He became quite a celebrity in all the newspapers and on television.

He was very grateful to Sarah for suggesting the place. She pretended her dog Bingo had been digging there and had discovered the hiding place.

Con was surprised when he developed the photos of the concert. All of them had turned out except the one of the boy. The picture was streaked with rainbow light. Sarah asked for it anyway.

Fr Sheppard and the Reverend Jones wrote several pamphlets, inspired, they said, by their conversations with the boy.

The committee agreed to have a small sculpture of an

angel placed in the grounds of the hospital. The children spoke about the boy for a long time afterwards.

Sergeant Thorpe never managed to track down Dr. Ahriman. Joe was brought to trial but was acquitted of manslaughter. Accidental death was the verdict, although no body was ever recovered. Joe never used the shotgun again.

Sarah's scar vanished, and her father and herself became great friends. Gran often mentioned the boy with affection and Jamie and Mary included him always in their prayers.

Sarah kept the wooden carving of the boy and dolphin and the photograph, along with her mother's photo, on her bedroom locker.

Just before going to sleep she would run her hand along the carving. She felt somehow he was still among them.

Also by Don Conroy

THE WINGS WILDLIFE FANTASY TRILOGY

ON SILENT WINGS
Illus. Don Conroy

Kos, a young and inexperienced barn owl, is left alone and terrified when his mother is killed by a hunter's trap. As he fights to survive he is helped by animals of the woodland, who know the constant dangers that surround them. But a new evil threatens to destroy them all – the rat Fericul and his monstrous army, who plan to take over the world. Can no one stand against them?

Paperback £4.99

WILD WINGS
Illus. Don Conroy

Vega, a kestral, begins life trapped in a falconry. His owl friend encourages him to escape and seek the freedom of the skies. But the world is under threat from the gang of rats who have escaped from a laboratory. Can Vega and his friends from the woodlands save the world from being thrust into permanent darkness?

Paperback £4.50

SKY WINGS
Illus. Don Conroy

The Feather of Light held at the Sacred Cliffs is the protector of the light of the world. A young falcon, Sacer, must try to take it to the darkness of Ratland in an attempt to wipe out the forces of darkness and evil once and for all.

Paperback £4.50

CARTOON FUN
With Don Conroy

Draw your own cartoons and get excellent results – faces, people, animals, comic strips, super heroes, monsters, dinosaurs, birds. Easy-to-follow instructions and great fun. It *really* works!

Paperback £4.99

WILDLIFE FUN
With Don Conroy

How to create lively and true-to-life drawings as well as cartoon animals. Failsafe instructions and models to follow. Includes lots of information on the lives of the animals. Full of fascinating fun.

Paperback £4.99

Send for our full colour catalogue